Jules is delighted when a contact at the BBC decides to make a documentary about the sixth form at St Andrews Road School. Of course, as presenter, he is obsessed with his appearance and fairly uninterested in the content of the programme. Like all real stars of the screen.

Mrs Potter, the Head Teacher, starts showing an interest and Taz and Ella are keen to put across a pupil's view of the National Curriculum. If he is not careful, Jules will be upstaged by his colleagues. This could be a disaster for someone destined for fame.

This is the sixth book in the S.T.A.R.S. sequence. Every month there will be a new, self-contained story, all about the same group of sixth formers. S.T.A.R.S. is based on reality, taking you inside a modern London comprehensive. Join now. The common-room door is always open. Waiting for you . . .

Hunter Davies is an author, journalist and broadcaster. He has written over thirty books, ranging from biographies of the Beatles to William Wordsworth, and he wrote the 'Father's Day' column in *Punch* for ten years. He is the author of the *Flossie Teacake* stories and has also written a book for teenagers, *Saturday Night*. He has three children and lives in London.

When Will I Be Famous

?

HUNTER DAVIES

PENGUIN BOOKS

PENGUIN BOOKS

Published by the Penguin Group
27 Wrights Lane, London W 8 5 T Z, England
Viking Penguin Inc., 40 West 23rd Street, New York, New York 10010, U S A
Penguin Books Australia Ltd, Ringwood, Victoria, Australia
Penguin Books Canada Ltd, 2801 John Street, Markham, Ontario, Canada L 3 R 1 B 4
Penguin Books (N Z) Ltd, 182–190 Wairau Road, Auckland 10, New Zealand

Penguin Books Ltd, Registered Offices: Harmondsworth, Middlesex, England

First published 1990
1 3 5 7 9 10 8 6 4 2

Text copyright © Hunter Davies, 1990
Photographs copyright © Ian O'Leary, 1990
Map copyright © Keith Brumpton, 1989
All rights reserved

Filmset in Linotron Ehrhardt by
Rowland Phototypesetting Ltd, Bury St Edmunds, Suffolk
Printed and bound in Great Britain by
Cox and Wyman Ltd, Reading, Berks.

Lukes Book

Jules: exhausted already

EPISODE 1

Jules's home, early morning

It's 8 January, first day of the new term, first day of a new year which is about to begin at St Andrews Road School. Jules is getting ready to meet the day, and the demands of another term. Major decisions always have to be made, regardless of what day or what year it is. Such as what to wear.

He throws off his duvet and goes to the large double-glazed windows to test the day, find out if there is weather out there. In the distance, he can see the white-spattered, criss-crossed slopes of Hampstead Heath, easy to spot at this time of the year, when the trees are bare. There are kids already rushing about, throwing snowballs, though the heavy drifts which fell over the New Year have almost gone. The morning is bright and crisp, with a hint of sun, but still very cold.

'Oh, God,' thinks Jules. 'I feel freezing just

looking at them. And how come they've got so much energy. I'm exhausted already.' He shivers. His room, like the rest of the flat, is at the same sub-tropical temperature all the year round. He goes back to bed, to recover his strength.

Jules loves the sixth form. From the moment he went into it, he felt at home. Life is different in the Sixth. The staff behave differently. The students seem different. People he never used to like, or dismissed as boring or thick, have somehow changed, turning out to have personalities, talents, skills, ideas. They have come through, emerged from their chrysalis and become themselves, just as Jules has done.

He lies in bed, thinking back, remembering how he felt displaced at so many stages lower down the school. There were rough times in the third year when he was picked upon, lonely times in the fourth year when he seemed out of things, dreary days in the fifth year when he hated several of his subjects. It now seems centuries ago. Throughout it all, he has managed to stay with the same nucleus of friends, most of them from his primary school.

These days, there are so many things to look forward to. Seeing the said friends, that's the first one. They were last all together at the New Year's Eve party at Sam's house. Then there's going back to the sixth-form common room. That should be in operation again today. It was closed most of last term, after certain parties had a certain party. The builders and decorators should have finished everything over the holidays.

'Tweed. I think my tweed jacket today. A bit of old-fashioned style is called for on a cold and frosty morning.'

Jules is still lying in bed, gazing at the window. Then he turns towards the stripped-pine wardrobe and groans. His father gave it to him last year, on his seventeenth birthday, having bought it at Camden Lock. Jules has moaned for three years now about the lack of space for his clothes.

'He's so mean. He knew I wanted my own dressing room, not a naff wardrobe. That's the first thing I'll do, when I'm rich and famous, even richer and more famous than I am now. I'll have two dressing rooms, one for winter clothes, one for summer.

'How anyone could buy that monstrosity. I suppose it could be worse, and have louvred doors. Yuck! He thinks it's ever so tasteful of course, being old and pine. He hasn't moved on since the sixties. Ugh. It looks like something out of, I dunno, Habitat.'

Jules smiles, having found the worst insult he can think of, and slowly gets up.

'If I'm late, it'll be her fault. Why hasn't she shouted for me yet? Silly woman.'

Jules's father is away on business, as he so often is, but he relies on his mother to get him up each morning in time for school. Jules has always found this very hard. Arriving on time for anything is a problem, even when it's something he is looking forward to, such as school today. He puts on his best tweed jacket, a secondhand one, of course. No one with any taste buys new clothes. It's real Harris tweed, bought for £25 at a shop in Covent Garden which only sells secondhand real Harris-tweed jackets.

'Hi, Mum,' he shouts, going into the breakfast room. 'I'm up.'

Before waiting for any reply, Jules suddenly returns to his bedroom. 'I must be wandering in my old age. They've seen this jacket. I wore it when I went round to Sam's to watch that video. Can't wear it again, not on the first day of term.'

He goes to his wardrobe, winces, then gets out a suit, dark-blue, pinstriped, double-breasted, circa 1955, bought in Camden Town, price £52. He's been looking forward to wearing this as he's thought of some amusing accessories. It takes time to get into this ensemble, as it means first putting on a light-blue polo neck, then a sparkling white shirt over that, leaving the first few buttons undone. Next comes the suit itself, making sure to fold down carefully the collar of the shirt over the suit lapels. That's the master stroke. Executive, but amusing.

Jules goes back to the breakfast room, ready to stun his mother, quite pleased he didn't see her before. She does tend to ridicule too many changes.

'Hi, Mum. Be prepared to be amazed. Taran–ta–ra . . .'

There is no one there. Propped up on the breakfast bar against the large glass jar of home-made muesli is a note he hadn't noticed earlier: 'Had to go in early. I'm a SOD today. Don't leave a mess.'

Jules sighs. She might have shouted for him, though perhaps she did and he didn't hear. He peels a banana, slices it into his muesli, pours on milk and then props up the *Independent*. He eats and reads at the same time most mornings, but today he finds this more difficult. He happens to be standing. This is in order to keep the creases in his suit. It doesn't work, holding the muesli bowl in one hand, while bending down to turn the pages of the *Independent* with the other, and trying to stop any dribbles from reaching his sparkling white shirt.

'Hmm, which shall I abandon? They're both healthy fodder, full of unadulterated fibre, nothing to upset the middle-class tum or the middle-class mind . . .'

He puts down the *Independent* and finishes his muesli, walking round the breakfast room. He notices his mother's note and reads it again. Jules must always have something to read, whether eating, travelling, or on the lavatory.

'It was better when she was just an ordinary social worker. She came home any time then, to do her supposed "write-ups". I wish she'd never been promoted. I fear I am now being neglected. Perhaps I should have my own social worker.'

Jules's mother is a team leader, a senior one, in line for further promotion, which explains why she often has to go into work early.

'Sod it. That's the third time she's been a SOD this week. Wait till I see her tonight.' SOD means Senior On Duty. Jules has picked up all the jargon. When his mother pokes fun at him about his clothes obsession, he replies by ridiculing her social-work terminology.

He puts his dirty bowl in the dishwasher, looks around, checks there is nothing that can be described as a mess, then leaves the flat.

'I won't need books today, not on the first day of term. Anyway, how can I carry stuff in a plastic carrier bag, wearing a suit? Just wouldn't go. Simply not on, old chap.'

He goes down in the lift, only four floors down, but Jules likes to save his energy. The block is not very big, just five storeys, ultra-modern with silent, carpeted corridors, linen-lined walls, burglar alarms and spy-holes everywhere, and a complicated intercom system at the front entrance.

Jules steps out, then steps in again. It is now snowing.

'Oh my God, I can't wear a suit in this. Listen, oh my God, I wish you'd stop it. I go to all this trouble, then you bugger it up with the weather. Do make up your mind, dear.'

He goes back upstairs, straight to his wardrobe, and this time puts on something more sensible, something more suitable for a comprehensive lower sixth former.

'Well, I suppose it would have been wasted anyway, on that shower. No style, any of them.'

He is now dressed in a black leather jacket, always a safe item, and jeans.

'This will give the common room a chance. Don't want to clash with any new colour schemes they might have inflicted upon us, do I.'

Jules is just leaving the flat when he notices the answerphone is flashing, indicating that someone has recorded a message. He stops, thinks, assuming it is probably his mother telling him she'll be late, and what to make himself for supper. He nearly doesn't listen to the message, but finally decides to.

'This is Simon here, and I want to leave a message for Jules. Hope this is still his number. Very simple – can he ring me? It's urgent. Thanks.'

St Andrews Road, fifteen minutes later

Jules has his head down, hurrying along. He started off wearing his shades, but soon took them off when they got splattered with snow.

'I should have booked a taxi. The wrinklies would go spare, but what the hell, this is an emergency. My Oliver Goldsmith frames could be ruined in this weather.'

Jules's father has a credit account with a taxi firm, as he has with various other businesses. Jules is allowed to use most of these accounts, if absolutely necessary. Often, he doesn't see his father for weeks on end. Instead, they correspond through Visa stubs, American Express bills, Access statements and sometimes, in a real emergency, through his father's accountant.

An old car, very much a banger, coughing and spluttering, clanking and creaking, grinds to a gradual halt beside Jules, sliding the last few metres on its shiny, bald tyres. Jules hurries on. He presumes it will be some idiot who is lost, wanting to know the way to Camden Town, or more likely,

Highgate. Everyone always gets that one-way system wrong.

'Gerrin, man,' says a voice.

'What?' shouts Jules. The car's silencer has gone and it sounds like a racing engine.

'I can't turn the bloody engine off,' grunts a voice. 'It'll never start again. So hurry up, man, if you wanna lift.'

Jules looks into the frosted-up windows, seeing nothing which resembles a human form. The front passenger door opens, then it falls downwards towards the kerb, before being hauled back in again and tied up with wire by the driver. While the door was open, Jules caught a quick glimpse of this same driver. He recognizes the mass of thick, matted, red hair, almost down to the waist, and the gold-rimmed specs.

'Matt,' he says. 'Didn't know you had a car.'

Jules grabs the passenger door, trying to open it, but a loud shouting and banging comes from inside, and eventually the rear door opens.

'Hurry up, man,' grunts Matt. 'We're gonna be late.'

The car accelerates away before Jules has properly climbed inside, veering across the road, skidding and sliding through the queues, while buses and cars all hoot their horns. Matt had crossed the road, against the traffic, just to give Jules a lift, which was very kind.

'Didn't know you could drive, either,' says Jules. 'That's if you *can* drive.'

All around, people are waving and shouting at

Matt. His eyes are focused on about ten centimetres of unfrosted window in front of him, a porthole on the world, periscope for his mind. While the eyes are busy on the traffic, the body below is swaying, feet banging from side to side. He has rigged up a primitive stereo, with wires everywhere and bashed-up speakers nailed to the seats. The noise is efficient and modern enough, though. Heavy Metal, of course. That's all Matt has ever really liked.

Matt is in the same tutor group as Jules. He's been with these friends all through school so far, but in a peripheral way, mainly because he lives in his own little world, apparently neither needing nor seeking close companions. For months he was in a squat, chucked out by his parents because of his music, but recently he has moved back home.

'Have you, er, passed your test?' asks Jules, as Matt swerves to avoid a bollard in the middle of a pedestrian crossing, then goes round the wrong side of it.

Jules can be outrageous in his style, and often in his conversation, but deep down, he is a law-abiding citizen, never wishing knowingly to transgress. Nor would he ever take any dangerous risks, not with his body or his clothes.

'Yeah, just passed, man – first time,' says Matt.

Jules has thought of getting a provisional licence now that he's seventeen, just for show, but his heart is not in it. He is completely unmechanical.

'Very good,' says Jules. *'Très bon.'*

'Don't you fancy it, man?'

'Not really,' says Jules. 'I've noticed one thing about all the upper sixth people who have cars.'

'What's that?'

'Dirty fingernails.'

Jules gives a little shudder, putting it on. This is part of his act, his self-created persona. At one time, when he was lower down the school, his mannerisms often had the wrong effect. People didn't see the joke and missed the self-mockery.

Matt smiles, then turns up the volume, banging his head as well as his feet and body. He appears to be putting his head through some very complicated manoeuvres, round and round, further and further out, straining all his neck muscles in unnatural contortions, as if trying to unscrew his head. Jules fears that it will come off, which would be inconvenient, as he has neither medical nor mechanical knowledge. A sudden image makes him smile: being forced to lean over and steer the car, with a headless Matt sitting in the driver's seat, still swaying to the strains of Iron Maiden.

He starts to tell Matt about this, knowing it will amuse him, as all Heavy Metallers love anything to do with death, judging by the skulls they scrawl on their exercise books, or have tattooed on their arms. But Matt can't hear. The music is too loud. Matt eventually turns it down, remembering Jules is behind him, and could even be addressing him.

'So,' says Jules, looking for some conversation to fill up the comparative silence. 'How's it going, Matt?'

'Not bad,' says Matt. 'I think it's going to work out

okay. I did have some trouble at first, getting started . . .'

Jules begins to regret his question, thinking that Matt is going to tell him all about his car, a subject he finds almost as boring as Heavy Metal.

'I meant the question generally,' says Jules quickly. 'Not your boring car. Life, the universe, the sixth form, and all that sort of stuff.'

'That's what I'm gonna tell you, man. I've made a big discovery.'

'That's good,' says Jules, rubbing the window, hoping to see where they are in St Andrews Road. It is a very long road but they should be almost at school. And the sooner the better.

'Maths is beautiful,' says Matt.

'You what?' says Jules. It's a phrase he never normally uses, considering it banal.

'Maths,' says Matt. 'Absolutely beautiful.'

Jules stops rubbing the window, wondering if he has heard correctly.

'It's the only subject worth studying in the whole world,' says Matt. 'Because it's the purest.'

'Is that so?' asks Jules, looking at Matt, checking he is not high on any funny substances.

'Physics and Chemistry, History or Geography, they're all sort of finite. You spend your time sort of summing up, pinning them down. Maths is infinite.'

'Really,' says Jules, wondering if he should get out of the car now.

'The Greeks realized it first. They're still number one, you know. No one's got higher in the charts than the Greeks. When old Euclid spoke about points and lines, he was talking about idealized entities, a point that has no dimension, a line that has no width, know what I mean? We're still trying to grasp all that. Have you got my drift, Jules?'

'Er, sort of.'

'You know about prime numbers, man?'

'Ye-es,' says Jules.

'They're numbers that you can't divide equally, unless you divide them by themselves or the number one. Like 2, 3, 5, 7, 11, 17 . . .'

'Ah yes,' says Jules, nodding his head, trying to appear knowledgeable. '19, 23, and, er, so on.'

'Yeah, but how far does the "so on" go?'

'Excuse me?'

'I mean, what's the largest prime number you can get?'

'Search me,' says Jules. 'I only got a C at GCSE.'

'That's it,' says Matt. 'The largest prime number known to man at the moment is a 65,050 digit number formed by raising 2 to the 216,091th power and subtracting one. Euclid said there are infinitely more. And we're still looking. He was the governor, he sussed it all out.'

Jules suddenly feels very ignorant. He has gone through school priding himself on his knowledge and love of languages, especially French and English, considering all scientists to be uncouth, unclever, uncultured. It's the sixth form that does it, he thinks. It brings them out, brings them on, like a hothouse.

Raffy: nice and clean

EPISODE 2

St Andrews Road School,
tutor room

The members of Mr Grott's tutor group are arriving, shrieking, shouting, kissing and cuddling, as if they haven't seen each other for decades. All of them did meet eight days ago at Sam's New Year's Eve party, though since then, Sam himself has been in the Lake District with his family, while Toby has been skiing for a week with his parents. The others have been hanging about in London in constant contact on the phone or visiting each other, while at the same time trying to get some work done after all the parties.

'What's new?' says Raffy to Jules.

'Not a lot,' says Jules.

'That's true,' says Raffy. 'I recognize that jacket.

A bit like Dim's, only not as big. It's not Colette's, is it? She used to have a leather jacket like that.'

'What?' says Jules, pretending he has not heard, busy giving Kirsty a big hug. 'Oh, this old thing. Had it yonkers. It's going to the National Theatre Museum when I've finished with it. You know it used to belong to John Lennon, when he was a rocker in Hamburg?'

Raffy pauses, not sure if this is a lie or not. Jules's father is known for his smart contacts.

'Have you heard about Matt?' says Kirsty to Raffy, giving him the slightest kiss, a hello kiss, not to be over-interpreted. She's being rather cool towards him since he got on so well with Taz at the New Year's Eve party. Mind you, she and Toby were very friendly then, too, though they're just friends again now. 'He's got a car. The first in the whole lower sixth to have his own car. Brilliant, isn't it?'

'No, sad, really,' says Raffy. 'But just typical of the middle classes. They have everything. Money, contacts, opportunities. I feel sorry for their children. What is there left for them to achieve in this world?'

'Oh belt up, Raffy,' says Colette. 'You're just jealous.'

'Anyway, Matt's not well off,' says Kirsty. 'His parents won't give him anything. He's just saved his money, instead of wasting it on beer or football, like some people I know.'

'Yeah,' says Colette. 'When he was in that squat, he was really poor.'

'What are you two on about?' says Raffy. 'Squats are full of middle-class kids. You can tell them a mile away. They all look like Matt: scruffy, dirty hair and torn jeans, just to show they don't care. They're all ashamed of their background, so they dress down, trying to be one of the plebs. You can tell the real working classes because they're so clean. Like you and me, Kirsty. Hmm, smell her, she's lovely.'

'Gerroff, pig,' says Kirsty, pushing him away.

'Well, I'm clean,' says Raffy. 'And I don't care who knows it.'

He jumps on a table and pulls open his shirt. 'Look at this chest. Every hair individually washed. Touch this flesh, girls, thrill to the pure goodness. And what about these underpants, pristine and virginal, just like little me . . .'

'Yeah, little's the word,' says Kirsty, sniggering, and Colette joins in. They're both putting it on, going into their *Blind Date* routine, imitating Cilla Black, shouting 'Worralad', and 'Worralotafun'.

Raffy is still prancing about, when two more people enter the tutor room. Taz, the beautiful Taz, now a good friend of Raffy's, or so he thinks, and Mrs Buttock, the school secretary. Raffy quickly jumps down, not wishing to be seen by Taz being vulgar and flash. She goes straight to Ella, who is standing at her locker, to tell her something about the School Council. Mrs Buttock doesn't look at Raffy either, going over to Mr Grott to give him a note.

'Thank you, Raffy,' says Mr Grott, standing up. 'A very good performance, but I think all the parts for exhibitionists have been cast so far.'

'Ha ha,' says Raffy.

'Jules, before you rush off,' continues Mr Grott, 'there's a message for you. And we would all be obliged if in future you could get your social secretary to handle your affairs, rather than making Mrs Buttock run round the school. She does have more important things to do.'

As they all go out to their first lesson, Mr Grott hands Jules a note. All it says is 'Ring Simon'.

The hall, later that morning

Mr Witting, Head of the Sixth, is in the middle of one of his regular pep talks to the whole sixth form, lower and upper. He goes through the excitements of the term ahead, important dates for the diary, vital things they must not forget. Naturally, everyone is slumped, pretending to be asleep or affecting deep boredom.

'And for those lower sixth formers doing A levels, which applies to half of you, don't forget there will be several opportunities to visit universities between now and the summer. The first visit, I think, will be to Sussex, but Miss Kling will give you further details in due course. There could be a free bus.'

'Wow,' says Raffy loudly, sitting at the back with his group. 'The things universities offer you these days, just to join them. Wait till the Midland Bank hears. Better than a rotten plastic wallet.'

Several people tell Raffy to shush, complaining that he's woken them up.

'Later in the term,' continues Mr Witting, 'we are likely to be closed for one if not two days while our masters instruct us in the new National Curriculum.'

'Makes a change from industrial action,' says Ella, bitterly.

'As you doubtless know,' says Mr Witting, 'the nation's eight million school pupils are going to have to follow this so-called National Curriculum, as decreed in the new Education Act recently passed by Parliament. We have still to know what delights are in store for us and for you, so at some time, the inspectors and the local authority officials will be gathering all staff together, to let us know what they think is going on.'

'Cut the irony, Lionel,' says Jules. 'You can't manage it.'

'Now for some good news,' says Mr Witting. 'I'm pleased to tell you that the common room will be open again, as from this lunchtime. New carpets have been laid, and I don't have to tell you we want them properly looked after. We have also had several fine specimens of tropical plants kindly donated by the PTA.'

'Marijuana, I hope,' says Raffy.

'And Mrs Potter has agreed that a table-tennis table can be bought, out of the School Fund.'

'Jolly, jolly good,' says Raffy. 'So we're being turned into a church youth club.'

'At our expense,' says Dim.

'Yeah, they soon forget, don't they,' says Raffy.

'Just as well, Raffy,' says Ella, poking him in the ribs.

The reason the common room has had to be

refurbished is because of damage caused during the party after a football match, in which Raffy was a prime culprit. Thanks to Dim's fund-raising efforts, the Sixth themselves found most of the money for the repairs.

'I might as well tell you the date for the first staff meeting of the term. From now on, of course, your representative will be attending.' Mr Witting searches amongst his papers, then reads out the date.

'And I think that's all,' he concludes, at which point everyone jumps up, proving they have been awake all the time.

'Except, oh, hold on, Miss Kling has asked me to say that Jules is wanted urgently by someone called Simon. He's been phoning the school all morning.'

There are yells and jeers all round. People go 'Ooooh' in high-pitched voices, or shout 'Ducky' and 'Get Jules', as they all push and shove to get out, heading for the common room.

Sixth-form common room, lunchtime

It's like the first day of the Royal Academy Summer Exhibition. Friends only, public not admitted. Everyone is going round examining the décor, the carpets, the colour scheme, the couches, the chairs, and oh my God, the plants.

And, like spectators at the first private viewing of a very special art show, they are all guzzling. Some have been to the canteen to get their midday victuals, while others are unpacking their home-made sandwiches.

'Those plants are just so vulgar,' says Jules. 'Why did they have to get such disgusting things. Don't they know that rubber plants and busy lizzies are revolting. We might as well have gladioli and be done with it.'

'And what's happened to our old battered sofa?' says Ella. 'I'm not sitting on that new monstrosity.'

'Perhaps you're meant to lie on it,' says Raffy, trying to pull it apart. 'I bet it's a sofabed. Come on, Ella, we'll try it out together. You're probably meant to lay on it. Lay, gerrit? Okay, we'll just try it for sighs, *sighs*, size . . .'

'Not that joke again,' says Kirsty. 'It wasn't funny when you cracked it in the second year.'

'At least they've got a new mirror for me,' says Jules, admiring himself, checking out his reflection. 'But I do think they might have cleaned it properly.'

'Perhaps they could clean you next time,' says Raffy. 'Get rid of those nasty stains, caused by too much self-absorption. Is there such a word? What do you think, Taz?'

'I think you're quite right,' smiles Taz, 'as always. Anyway, Ella, what do you think I should bring up at the first staff meeting?'

Jules thinks the mirror is his as it was he who organized a petition to have one installed, back in the early weeks of the first term. He examines his reflection from all corners of the room, working out where best to position himself for the rest of his sixth-form life.

Colette and Kirsty have bagged the new couch and settled themselves down, sprawling all over it.

23

They save a place for Ella, when she has finished her serious chat with Taz. 'I always thought Matt was lovely,' says Colette. 'Don't you think, Kirst?'

'Ever so sweet,' says Kirsty. 'Where is he, anyway?'

'He's moving his car,' says Colette. 'Trying to find a better place to park it. Old fishface won't let him bring it on school property. Staff only.'

'Oh, poor Matty.'

'He's so sweet,' says Colette.

'What a couple of scrags you are,' says Raffy, bouncing down on the couch, forcing himself between them. 'Just cos he's got a car. I've got something much more exciting, which I know you'd both love to have a ride on . . .'

'Who's your friend?' says Kirsty.

'Dunno,' says Colette. 'Some vulgar lout. I think he was responsible for the plants, don't you, Jules? Anyway, gerroff, you pig!'

Kirsty and Colette together push Raffy as hard as they can with their legs, till he slowly slides off on to the floor.

'Not a bad carpet,' says Raffy. 'Bags me this spot. I'll lie here. Let me wilt on the Wilton, let me die a young man's death, a between-the-sheets death. Jules, what's the rest of that verse? Is it Shakespeare or Roger McGough?'

'Actually, it's not bad,' says Jules. 'They've done quite a good job, considering.'

'Considering they never consulted us,' says Ella, sitting down in her place on the couch. 'You would have thought they would have consulted some of us about the décor and the fittings, as we are the consumers. We have to live here. And we supplied the money, too.'

'Talking about death,' says Raffy, still lying on the floor, 'my first and only memory of my mother is about death. We were at the seaside one day, Brighton, or Southend, or somewhere. Dunno where. I must have been about seven. And I was like all little kids of that age, I thought I would never die. Then it just struck me, wham, as we were in this amusement arcade. I can see it so clearly. I was about to roll these pennies, when I suddenly burst into tears, screaming, "I'm going to die, I'm going to die."'

There is a sudden silence from the people immediately around Raffy. Elsewhere, the hubbub continues, the chats and exclamations, the shouts and shrieks. But on the couch, they are rather moved by Raffy's memory, though they don't want to admit it.

'Do you mind, Raffy?' says Kirsty. 'Not on the first day of term. Can't you think of something less morbid to talk about?'

'Yeah, give us a break, Raf,' says Colette. 'This is a happy day.'

'Not my fault,' says Raffy. 'That's how God created it. Or whoever. Some bimbo, some dum dum, some right wally. Pretty stupid, you must admit, whoever thought it all up. Life has got such a corny plot, if you ask me. I could have done better.'

'In that case,' says Jules, 'you must welcome death.'

'How do you mean, Jules?' says Raffy, turning on his side to face Jules, pleased to have someone willing to listen to him and humour him.

'Well, the sooner you die, the sooner you defy his plans. If, of course, you do sincerely think they are stupid and silly.'

'Oh, I do,' says Raffy. 'Absolutely potty. But I've decided to hang on, make the most of it, get the best out of it. Gather ye rosebuds while ye may. Now who said that, Jules, eh? It's one of my gran's favourites, which is pretty daft, as she's gathered bugger-all in her seventy-nine years, except a load of old wrinkles and a very small pension.'

'Robert Herrick,' says Jules. 'Seventeenth-century poet. He also wrote "Cherry Ripe".'

'Well, what do you know,' says Raffy.

'Look, can you two intellectuals give us a break?' says Sam. 'I am trying to have my lunch in peace.'

'Yeah, and I am trying to read,' says Dim, examining *The Financial Times*.

'And I am trying to write,' says Taz, her best Waterman pen in her hand.

'Oh gosh, what busy bees,' says Raffy. 'It's so good to be back amongst all this brainpower.'

Into the common room staggers Matt, all covered in grease and dirt. Kirsty and Colette jump up at once, rushing to see he is all right, offering to fetch cloths and water to dampen his fevered brow.

'Is it okay?' asks Kirsty.

'Have you managed to park it?' asks Colette.

Matt grunts, pushing past them towards Jules.

He digs deep in his pocket and brings out a crumpled note, also covered in grease.

'This is for you. Mr Banks gave it to me as I came in. You have to ring someone. I dunno, Mr Simon or something, know what I mean. The initials are Bee Bee something.'

'Not again,' groans Raffy. 'You've organized all this, haven't you, Jules? Just to be flash, having people ringing you all day long. What a show-off.'

'BBC!' says Jules. 'Of course. Thanks, Matt.'

'Oh God,' says Raffy, 'here he goes again. What a poser.'

'Taz, my darling,' says Jules. 'As you have your clipboard ready, five things to bring up at the staff meeting.'

'Yes, Jules,' says Taz, smiling. 'Fire away.'

'One, proper car-parking facilities on the school premises for all members of the sixth form. Two, the Jules Memorial Mirror to be cleaned every morning, for ever. Three, all discussions from henceforth pertaining to the new curriculum to involve members of the student body, as we are the primary consumers. Four, it is absolutely vital that all vulgar plants be removed from the sixth-form common room, forthwith. Five, we want a payphone for use by all sixth formers, especially those being pursued by the media. Oh, it's just so boring, being famous . . .'

'Oh shurrup, Jules,' says everyone.

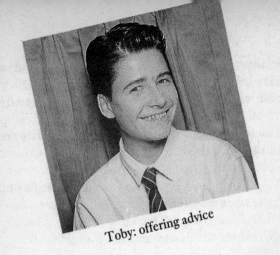

Toby: offering advice

EPISODE 3

Cow and Bull, next day,
early evening

The friends are all sitting, waiting impatiently. They have drunk their modest drinks quickly, expecting to have only a few minutes to put in before Jules turned up. He was due half an hour ago.

'Typical,' says Ella. 'He's never been on time in his life. I'm giving him ten more minutes, then I'm going home. I've got work to do.'

'So have I,' says Colette, mournfully, 'if only I could do it. I think I'll give up French. There's no point in it. Not with her.'

They all groan, looking for some distraction. Raffy goes to the space invader machine, jiggling it, kicking it, hoping to make it work, *sans* dosh. Sam looks at the jukebox, willing something good to come on. Dim takes out a crumpled copy of the School Bulletin and starts to read it.

'She hates me, that's the real reason,' says Colette.

Even Kirsty and Ella, always so loyal to Colette, give little sighs. She is going on a bit.

'And she's useless. I can't even understand what she's saying when she's speaking English.'

'Have you been to see Mr Witting?' says Toby. 'Try and get a different teacher.'

'They're short. You can't get language teachers, that's the trouble. It's her or nothing.'

'What do Jules and Taz think about her?' asks Toby. They are also in Colette's French group, but neither is present in the pub, so far. Taz is not really expected, though she has been invited.

'Jules is brilliant,' says Colette, 'so it doesn't matter to him, and Taz gets extra coaching. She's always in France anyway, with her dad, so her accent is terrific.'

'I wish I could get extra coaching for my Geography,' says Sam. 'My rotten parents won't allow it. That bloke we have is a right idiot. And he doesn't like me.'

'Oh God, give us a break,' says Raffy, returning. 'What a lot of old moaners. Thought this was gonna be a good night, with old Jules bringing us some exciting news. What time was he supposed to be at the BBC, anyway?'

'Four o'clock,' says Ella. 'Straight from school. Then he said he'd come here at six, and tell us all the gen. Right, five minutes, then that's it.'

'Hey, this is interesting,' says Dim, pointing at a paragraph in the Bulletin.

'Let us be the judge of that,' says Raffy.

They hardly read the Bulletin, chucking it out the moment they are given their copy. It's only a two-page leaflet which comes out every week and is supposed to keep everyone up-to-date with school news. Mrs Potter began it when she took over as Head, to bring them all together, foster the community spirit.

Raffy grabs the paper from Dim's hand. 'Oh yeah, this is really fascinating, folks. Did you know that Elspeth Worthington, 5G, is going to play with the Camden Schools' Orchestra? Riveting, huh. And Gabrielle Papadopolou, 2H, was sixth in the London girls' cross-country championship and could, perhaps, don't get too excited, get into the under-thirteen London team! And look at this, man. Kirit Patel in 1B has won a meal for two at Fred's Caff in the PTA Grand Draw. Lucky beggar.

'Hold on, though, it's not all big news. Here's a little homily from the big chief herself. I think she wrote it specially for Jules's benefit.'

Raffy clears his throat and does a good imitation of Mrs Potter.

'PUNCTUALITY! That is one of the aims I have set all students this term. I would appreciate parents' support, as regards this. It is important that our students develop the habit of being punctual and learn to organize themselves properly so as to get here on time, some students were getting slack about this towards the end of last term. Now! is the time to make a new beginning!'

'God, she's illiterate, that woman,' says Ella. 'She doesn't know how to form sentences, or when not to use exclamation marks. How did she become Head?'

Dim takes the Bulletin back from Raffy and points to a paragraph at the bottom of the front page, which he then reads out.

'SIXTH-FORM TUCKSHOP. I am looking for someone, better still two people, to open a sixth-form tuckshop as a private enterprise venture. We can provide the kitchen and the customers. We need an entrepreneur, so if you know of anyone who would be interested in running a tuckshop in the common room from, say 11 a.m. to 2.00 p.m., five days a week, during term time, ask them to please contact the school.'

'Boring, boring,' says Raffy.

'I think it's a good idea,' says Colette. 'It's stupid having to trail to the main building for our food, then bring it back across the yard to our common room. We should have our own facilities. Especially with the new common room.'

'But who's going to take it on?' says Toby. 'Trusthouse Forte?'

'More like Fred's Caff,' says Raffy.

'We could do it, you know,' says Dim, thinking hard.

'Don't be daft, Dim,' says Colette. 'She wants a proper firm, an outside catering business.'

Dim gets up and goes to the bar where Neville, the manager, is wiping glasses. He can be heard asking Neville which cash and carry firm he uses, what sort of discount the pub gets, and how much a secondhand microwave oven might cost. Neville starts to answer, but is called away to the phone.

'I'm going,' says Ella, standing up.

'And me,' says Colette.

'Yeah, let's go,' says Sam, getting up too.

'It's for you,' shouts Neville, holding the phone. Everyone stops and looks round, wondering who he means.

'You're Sam, aren't you?' says Neville. 'Well, it's for you. And don't be bloody long. This is a private phone.'

Sam picks the receiver up, while the others crowd round him.

'Sam?' says a voice, clearly distinguishable as that of Jules. 'Where the hell are you all? I've been waiting here for ages.'

'Where are you?' asks Sam.

'Your place,' says Jules. 'That was the arrangement.'

'No it wasn't,' says Sam. 'You said the pub.'

'Don't be mad,' says Jules. 'I wouldn't arrange to meet in a public place like that. Anyone might overhear. Get round here at once. That's if you all sincerely want to be famous . . .'

Sam's bedroom, five minutes later

'Coffee,' shouts Jules, lying back on Sam's bed, looking autocratic, listening to them all rushing up the stairs. He is wearing shades and holding a clipboard.

They all rush in, led by Raffy, desperate to hear Jules's news.

'I said coffee,' says Jules.

'On your bike, Jules,' says Raffy. 'Come on, give.'

'Darlings,' says Jules, 'I can't possibly do a thing without coffee. And none of that instant rubbish either.'

'Okay then,' says Sam. 'For everyone? But don't start till I get back. Promise.'

Sam can be heard running down the stairs and into the kitchen. Jules gets up and wanders round the room, examining Sam's possessions, which he knows by heart anyway. Since the first year, they have all used Sam's house as a meeting place, being so near the school. Sam's mother has always encouraged it, welcoming all his friends.

Jules admires himself in a broken mirror, found on a skip, which is propped up on a bookshelf. Ella put it there in order to do her hair when she visits Sam. Sam himself always pretends he is not interested in his appearance, unlike some people he could mention.

'My God, this is appalling,' says Jules.

'Yeah, you're not looking so cool tonight, Jules,' says Raffy.

'I mean this stupid mirror. Why don't you make him get a full-length one, Ella?'

'He says he doesn't care,' says Ella.

'He'll have to,' says Jules, 'if I'm going to turn him into a superstar. And that applies to all of you.'

Raffy groans, furious at being teased and kept waiting. He turns on Sam's ghetto blaster, very loud. The sound of hammering on the wall comes from the next bedroom, where Sarah, Sam's younger sister, is doing her homework. Jules turns the music off. Raffy looks at him, smiles, but does nothing, knowing Jules is in the driving seat and is going to make the most of it. So Raffy lies down on the rug, pretending to snore, till Sam returns with the coffees.

'Right,' says Raffy, jumping up. 'Cut the bullshit, Jules. Just tell us, eh.'

'Well,' says Jules, 'I didn't realize who this Simon was at first, when he rang me. I'd forgotten those three days I did work shadowing last term, as they were just so boring. But obviously I made a huge impression on him. As I always do . . .'

'Cut the crap, Jules,' says Raffy.

'Do you remember work shadowing?' asks Jules. 'When Kirsty was in that photographer's, and Taz was at Marks. Toby was in that architect's place. Now where were you, Sam?'

'Give me strength,' says Raffy. 'Get on with it.'

'This BBC bloke, Simon, the one I shadowed, was working at BH at the time. Oh, sorry about that folks, technical language. It stands for Broadcasting House. You'll have to get used to the jargon when you're all mega in the media. BH is the BBC's HQ for the radio and the DG's office is there too. Oops, sorry, another one. Director General. Make notes if you like.'

Raffy picks up a pair of Sam's trainers and throws one at Jules, but he ducks in time.

'Simon was producing this dreary book programme on radio, but he's now been moved to TV, on secondment for six months. They're always doing that at the BBC, moving all the time, very confusing. When I rang him back at the number he'd left, no one seemed to know him.'

The second trainer flies through the air, this time hitting Jules on the arm and spilling his cup of coffee. They all shout at Raffy for being so stupid. Ella goes to the sink on the landing, gets a wet cloth and mops up the mess on the carpet. Jules is spinning the story out deliberately, mainly to annoy Raffy, whom he knows has always been besotted by the idea of being discovered, either through going on television or getting a part in a film. Raffy once planned to make it as a pop star, but things didn't quite work out. There were minor problems, such as not being able to sing or play any instrument.

'Simon's now in TV documentaries and he's setting up a programme on education. Naturally, he thought of me straight away. Anyway, he's just asked me to present it.'

'Liar,' says Raffy.

'Look, just tell it straight, Jules,' says Ella. 'Don't embroider things.'

'Well then, I won't tell you lot anything, if you're going to accuse me of making it all up. I think that's most unfair.'

'Okay, I apologize,' says Raffy.

'Before you all arrived,' says Jules, 'I was in fact

writing out a list. I've got to do little personal profiles of likely people, to hand over to Simon. But if you're all going to be horrible, I'll think of other people to appear in *my* programme.'

'Jules, is this on the level or not?' asks Toby.

'Of course it is. Would I lie? Simon wants me to suggest people who could appear in this programme. I'm not supposed to let you see my notes. I just have to pass them on to him, informally, so he can make up his mind, then he'll talk directly to the people he likes the sound of. He wants strong personalities, typical comprehensive sixth formers, who'll be fluent and natural.'

'That's me,' says Raffy. 'I'll be gold-dust.'

'Yes, I think you are still on my list,' says Jules, looking at his notes. 'So far. I did have Matt down as well, but really, he's not very fluent.'

'Oh, poor Matt,' says Kirsty.

'He's so sweet,' says Colette.

'And I've crossed out Vinny,' continues Jules. 'I don't think it will do St Andrews any favours to have yobs appearing, apart from you, Raffy. One is enough.'

'Am I on your list, Jules darling?' asks Colette, going over to the bed and trying to see his notes.

'Let me see. Yes! Now, isn't that funny. By an amazing coincidence, I have only to suggest eight names at this stage, a good sort of cross section, and I happen to have rejected every other person in the entire sixth form, except my eight closest and dearest friends. Now, isn't that strange?'

'Thanks, Jules,' says Kirsty, giving him a kiss. 'I'd do the same for you.'

'Course, I don't know that Simon will choose all of you. That's up to him. And up to you to be *magnifico* when he meets you, and not be stupid or muck him around.'

'What about you, Jules?' asks Ella.

'I've told you,' says Jules, breathing on the backs of his fingers, then rubbing them on his shirt. 'I've *been* chosen. I'm going to be the star.'

'How much?' asks Dim.

'How much of a star?' asks Jules, raising his eyebrows, then holding out his arms. 'Oh, this big. Or bigger. Out of sight, I should think.'

'I mean, how much money? What's the fee?'

'Sometimes, Dim, you are just so sordid. This is your big chance to make it, and you're worrying about the money.'

'When's he want to see us?' asks Raffy.

'Soon as I give him this list. Photographs would probably help, so each of you give me a snap at school tomorrow.'

'I haven't got one,' says Ella.

'God, what will I wear?' says Kirsty.

'My hair's a mess,' says Colette.

'What about me, darling?' says Jules. 'I'm the star. *My* clothes will be crucial, absolutely crucial. I've got my public to think about. Ten million people will be out there, waiting to be astonished.'

'What's it about, this programme?' asks Toby.

'About half an hour, I think,' says Jules.

'I mean the subject, clever clogs.'

'Education. Life in a modern, urban comprehensive. Oh come on, you know. You've seen it before, the usual sort of stuff. But with one very big difference this time. It will be a world première performance, starring the one and only, *Jules* ... Closely followed, but not too closely, by Ella, Kirsty, Colette, Taz, Toby, Raffy, Sam and even Dim, if he wants to.'

'I'll fink about it,' says Dim. 'Where will he meet us, anyway?'

'Oh, Simon will take us all out somewhere posh,' says Jules. 'No *problema*. Probably the Groucho Club, that's where the media people meet, or perhaps a private room at the Savoy. I haven't been told yet. But these TV people do things in style. Don't you worry, my old son.'

Jules gets up from the bed, carefully tucking his notes away. 'I'll let you know the moment I hear from Simon. Keep in touch, okay yah?'

'Has it got a name, this programme?' asks Toby, as they all start to leave the bedroom. 'Or is it part of a series? I mean, like *Panorama*.'

'No, it's a one-off,' says Jules. 'They'll probably call it something like *The Changing Face of Education*.'

Immediately there are groans all round.

'Oh no, how bloody boring,' says Raffy. 'No one will watch it. How am I gonna be discovered in a crappy old documentary with some boring name?'

'Then don't appear,' says Jules. 'I can always get someone else. Matty, for example.'

'Okay, I suppose I will,' says Raffy.

'What you have to realize, fans,' says Jules, 'is that this is our chance. We must each of us use this to our advantage . . .'

Kirsty: devoted sister

EPISODE 4

Jules's home, one week later

Jules comes into the designer kitchen, sits at the breakfast bar, picks up the *Independent* and waits for his mother. She is on the phone, talking to the police.

'Come on, woman,' says Jules. 'I'm starving.'

'Hold on. Just one moment please, before you go any further,' his mother is saying on the phone, sounding rather irate, trying to get a word in. 'Exactly what address did you say?'

'Oh, hurry up,' moans Jules. 'It's the same every morning.' He looks at the jar of home-made muesli, then shoves it away with a groan.

'Ah, excuse me,' his mother is saying, her voice betraying a small sign of triumph. 'That is not us. That is Area Five. You'll have to try them . . . Not at all. Thank you.'

'I dunno,' says Jules, as his mother hangs up and joins him at the breakfast bar. 'Staff these days. When I'm a multi-millionaire media mogul, I'll insist that none of my staff takes personal calls during working hours.'

'I do happen to be working,' says his mother.

'You never stop,' says Jules.

'Typical of that sergeant. Just trying to dump kids on us, get them off his hands.'

Jules ignores this. He doesn't want to hear about his mother's work dramas. At the same time, she is ignoring all his references to his impending media-explosion drama.

'What are you waiting for, anyway, Lord Muck?' says his mother, noticing that the muesli jar is right across the counter. 'Too tired to put anything in your bowl, hmm? Too exhausted to pour out the milk? Too famous to even move, huh?'

She stands up, gets the jar and starts to pour some into a bowl for Jules.

'When I was your age, we got no breakfast –'

'Oh, don't start that,' says Jules. 'You went out on the beach at Ocho Rios and collected coconuts, I know. You drank the milk, and you've never been so fit in your life.'

'It's true,' she says.

'It's also true that you are ruining my health with all this rubbish food,' says Jules.

'What are you talking about?' says his mother, picking up the *Independent*.

'I'm wasting away. You're stunting my growth. Haven't you heard about muesli-belt malnutrition?'

'Is it a new group?'

'Ha ha,' says Jules. 'That just shows your ignorance. All teenagers need high-energy food to make them grow, but you are forcing this middle-aged faddy stuff on me. We don't need skimmed milk and muesli and low-fat tasteless stuff. That's for forty-five-years-olds, like Dad, to stop them having heart attacks.'

'Good,' says his mother turning the pages. 'So you'll be picking up good habits now, which will last you through life.'

'If I live that long,' says Jules. 'I won't make forty-five at this rate, on this rabbit junk.'

'Oh, I think you'll manage.'

'If I get anorexia, it will be your fault.'

'Don't think there's a high risk of that.'

'Look at my cheeks, they're caving in as it is. How am I gonna look on the television? I'll be like a skeleton soon, and it's all your fault.'

'Oh yes,' says his mother, still reading. 'How come?'

'You and Dad are the typical over-motivated, middle-class over-achievers. And I have to suffer for it. Ignored, deprived of affection and attention in my childhood, and now –'

'Not that one, Jules,' says his mother, sighing. 'You know perfectly well I never went back to work till you were eleven, not that that has anything to do with it, anyway.'

'And if all that wasn't bad enough, now you're trying to starve me.'

'Look, just eat up and shut up. You're going to be late.'

'Told you. Can't eat this rubbish. The only decent food I get is when I stay with Grandpa. He cooks ackee and salt fish, jerk pork and jerk chicken. Really tasty, filling stuff. I wish you'd never gone to Oxford, but stayed for ever in your mud hut in the jungle.'

His mother gets up and hits him over the head with the *Independent*, then empties the muesli back into the glass jar.

'Just get off to school.'

'Now she's sending me out on a freezing morning with nothing at all to eat.'

'So what is it you would like then? Tell me, pray.'

'Chips and crisps and chocolate, that'll do for a start. Just the normal sort of stuff which normal teenagers eat.'

'Oh great. Really healthy.'

'Did you know that crisps have three times as much vitamin C as an apple?'

'Save that for your TV interview,' says his mother, giving him a quick kiss as he leaves the room. 'Astound the nation, as I'm sure you will . . .'

Jules can still hear her laughing as he goes to the lift.

Kirsty's flat, near the top of a high-rise block

Her mother is rushing around, from the frying pan to the table, carrying huge plates of bacon and eggs which her husband and son Kevin are tucking into, one reading the *Daily Express* and the other the

Mirror. At the end of the table, their second television, a portable colour one, is blaring away, tuned
to TV-am.

'Oh come on, dear,' says her mother, seeing
Kirsty getting her bag ready. 'You can't go off to
school on just a glass of orange juice. It's not good
for you.'

'You mean it's not bad for you,' says Kirsty. 'Not
like that poison those pigs are shovelling down their
gobs.'

Kevin makes grunting noises, like a pig, and
shoves even more in his mouth. Too much, so that
some of his egg yolk drips over the plate and on to
the table. Her father doesn't even look up. He's not
at his best at breakfast.

Kirsty shrieks at him to stop it. Then Mandy, her
younger sister, joins in.

'Mandy, you haven't even had any orange juice,'
says their mother. 'What is going on?'

'Yeah,' grunts Kevin. 'She just copies Kirsty. It's
all her fault, Kirsty's. Tell her off, Mum.'

'I need some dinner money, Mum,' says Kirsty.

'What, dear?' says her mother, now back in the
kitchen. 'Can't hear you.'

'Turn that bloody thing off,' shouts Kirsty, going
and switching off the TV.

'Don't swear, Kirsty,' says her father.

'And I need money for the coach,' says
Mandy. 'We're going to sodding Kew Gardens
today.'

'Gotta keep it on, ain't we,' says Kevin, leering,
turning the TV back on. 'Just in case anything good

44

comes on, know what I mean. Like Kirsty and her poncy sixth-form friends, know what I mean.'

'Yes, dear,' says her mother, returning with a large pot of tea, enough to refresh a regiment. 'What *is* happening to your programme? Mrs Mayer was asking if she's missed it.'

'Hasn't been made yet,' says Kirsty. 'If it ever will get made.'

'I've told everyone in the block,' says her mother. 'They're all so excited.'

'Oh Gawd,' says Kirsty, 'why did I ever mention it?'

'Cos you're trying to be flash, that's why,' says Kevin.

'Shut your mouth,' says Kirsty. 'Right, if you haven't got any money, Mum, I'll have to do without lunch. Just as I've gone without breakfast.'

Her mother goes across to Kevin, wipes her hands on her apron and holds them out. Kevin delves into his boilersuit and brings out a wad of notes, peeling off one for his mother. She then hands it to Kirsty.

'And I want the change, mind,' she says.

'No chance,' snarls Kirsty. 'You owe me a bleedin' fortune.'

'Kirsty!' shouts her father.

'I hope you don't talk to your friends like that,' says her mother.

'Course not,' say Kevin. 'She just saves her bad temper for us, not her la-di-da friends.'

Kirsty bangs out, without saying cheerio, closely

followed by Mandy. On the concrete, open walk way, Kirsty turns and glares at Mandy.

'Yes?' says Mandy defiantly. 'You bothered?'

She has brushed back and gelled her blonde hair, in the same style as Kirsty, and has smeared her lips with cheap Woolworth's lipstick, just like Kirsty. Mandy is thirteen. Kirsty has always been responsible for taking her to school, right from primary days. And the same thought has always bugged her.

What Kirsty fears most is that total strangers will take her and Mandy for sisters.

Meanwhile, over at Sam's house

Sam is standing in the large, open pine kitchen, making his own breakfast, as always. This is known as free play in their house. Each person has to make their own breakfast: his mother, father and younger sister Sarah. His mother has already gone to work. Sarah went to school ages ago.

Sam is making toast, slice after slice, layering on the butter as if he's using a trowel, then smearing on marmalade by the spoonful. He eats as if in a dream, as he so often is. He is also staring out into the garden, gazing at the dead bushes, the bare pear trees, the frosty film across the lawn and thinking deep thoughts. Such as, what about the tortoise? How can it sleep all winter? What does it have for breakfast? He almost jumps in the air when someone appears behind him.

'What's that smell?' says his father, coming into the kitchen and switching on the kettle.

'Not me,' says Sam.

'Look, it's burning, you fool,' says his father, rushing to turn off the toaster.

'That's how I like it. Put it on again.'

'No, just wait till I've finished,' says his father.

'Mum said one at a time,' says Sam. 'You know the rules. Get out till *I've* finished. I was here first.'

'I hate you fussing in the kitchen,' says his father.

'You're the one who's fussing,' says Sam.

They push and shove each other, jostling for control of the breakfast things. Sam switches off his father's kettle. As retaliation, his father turns off Sam's coffee-machine.

'Look, get lost,' says Sam, 'I was first.'

'Don't be stupid, there's room for both of us.'

'Okay, then,' says Sam. 'I'll make coffee for both of us. I'll be kind to you, even if you are never kind to me.'

'Thanks, Sam,' says his father, picking up the *Guardian* and sitting down. 'I take tea now, not coffee, remember.'

'Oh yeah, your ulcers. How are they?'

'Don't talk about them.'

Sam makes his coffee really black and strong, letting it percolate for some time, the way he likes it, then he turns on the toaster for just one more slice. His father sniffs, glancing longingly at Sam's mug.

'Sure?' Sam asks his father, handing him his mug of tea.

'No thanks,' says his father.

'What do you think I should do about Geography?' asks Sam after a while.

'Geography?' says his father, still reading.

'You know, A levels, school,' says Sam. 'You've probably been wondering where I go every day. That big building round the corner, right on St Andrews Road. You can't miss it.'

'I did Geography A level,' says his father.

'That wasn't the question. Anyway, you were at a grammar school, back in the dark ages. It's all changed now.'

'Can't see why. Since Christopher Columbus, not a lot has changed, geography-wise.'

'We're doing map projections. I can't understand what the hell is going on.'

'Well, try harder,' says his father.

'Thanks a lot. You're a great help.'

'Good,' says his father, not listening.

'It's not my fault. We've got this rotten teacher. He thinks I'm stupid.'

'I wonder what makes him think that.'

'I might just give it up. Completely. Leave school and not do A levels.'

'Not a bad idea,' says his father, turning over the 'Appointments' pages. 'A lot of good jobs for labourers in today's paper.'

'This is serious. I honestly don't know what's happening.'

'Well, how about some private tuition, till you catch up?'

'Tell that to Mum,' says Sam. 'I suggested it to her, but she says over her dead body. If the teaching is bad, so she says, then we have all got to work together to improve it. One mustn't opt out, and other cobblers.'

'She's quite right,' says his father.

'You're a creep,' says Sam.

'Right again,' says his father, getting up and putting his dirty mug in the dishwasher.

'But how can you make things better? You can't just get rid of bad teachers, that's the problem. They won't listen to you.'

'Tell you what,' says his father. 'In this TV programme you're doing, if you're still doing it –?'

Sam nods.

'Why don't you talk about that? No need to name the actual Geography teacher, just the principle of it. It's a good topic for discussion. The Government says it wants teachers to be accountable, and bad teachers to be eased out.'

'Thanks, Dad,' says Sam. 'Sometimes you do have good ideas.'

Breakfast time in Colette's flat

Colette is still in bed, being pampered by her mother, who is preparing to bring her a boiled egg for her breakfast. The two of them live in a small flat in an old Edwardian house. The kitchen is hardly more than a galley, hidden by a bead curtain.

'Mum, you don't have to bother,' shouts Colette from her bed. 'Go on. You'll be late for work.'

'It's okay, darling. I can be later today, the boss is abroad. It's you I'm worried about. I don't want you going out with an empty stomach on a day like this. What time do you start, anyway?'

'Soon, soon,' says Colette. 'I've got two free periods.'

'I just don't understand this system. When I was in the sixth form, we had to be in school all the time.'

'Yes, Mother,' says Colette. She is turning over the pages of her mother's copy of *Vogue*. Her mother brings in a tray, complete with cloth and a little vase of freesias.

'Oh, isn't that sweet,' says Colette. 'Kissy, kissy.' She lifts her cheek up, so her mother can kiss her.

'Well, you are my favourite daughter,' says her mother. 'If the egg is too hard, just tell me, and I'll do another. Nothing is too good for a television star.'

Colette smiles indulgently, turning over the pages.

'Oh my God!' shrieks her mother, rushing out of the bedroom. 'I've forgotten the soldiers. They're still in the kitchen.'

'So that's where you keep them, eh? Well leave some for me. Me and Kirsty could do with a few. Better than all the wimps we normally have to make do with.'

Her mother returns with the hot toast, neatly cut into soldiers, oozing with butter.

'I remember this test we once had in the third year,' says Colette. 'We had to do this translation from the French and I mixed up *souliers* with *soldats*. It was about this old woman, and I said that before she went to sleep, she put a soldier under her bed, instead of her shoes under the bed.'

Colette's mother bursts out laughing, dropping the toast fingers on the floor.

'Oh, you dum dum,' says Colette. 'If you've ruined my new rug –'

'It's okay, okay,' says her mother. 'They didn't fall butter-side down. Now, that is a good sign. It must mean we're going to have a lucky day. Isn't it your TV meeting today, darling?'

'Could be,' says Colette. 'Jules is going to tell us.'

'Isn't it strange when you couldn't put on that play last term. Now, perhaps you're going to be a professional actress.'

Ella, Colette and Kirsty formed an unofficial sixth-form drama group the previous term, and worked really hard at a play they chose for themselves. The only snag was, Mrs Potter discovered it was set in a public lavatory, with a sanitary-towel incinerator, and banned it. Much to their disgust.

'It's only a documentary, Mum, not a feature film.'

'Well, you don't know where it might lead,' says her mother. 'Once everyone sees you in this documentary, who knows what might happen. You could be spotted. People are looking out for new young talent all the time. There are so many programmes these days. They've got to fill them somehow.'

'Thanks a lot, Mum.'

'I didn't mean it that way. I mean there are so many opportunities, especially living in London. You're just so lucky. I see TV crews in our area all the time. They were in Kentish Town yesterday, when I was coming home. And last week I saw a whole film crew on Hampstead Heath, with these huge refreshment lorries.'

'Give us a break, Mum. You're getting carried away.'

'In Carlisle, we never saw any TV or film people. We never spotted famous people in the street, the way you're always doing. Who was that weather forecaster you saw at Camden Lock on Saturday?'

'Mother, you're becoming boring.'

'The only famous person I ever knew in my whole life, when I was growing up, was the Mayor of Carlisle's daughter. She was in our sixth-form French class. We used to stand up every time she came into the room, just as a joke. We'd say "Arise, it's the Mayor's daughter." She must have hated it. I wonder where she is now . . .'

'Yes, I've often wondered myself,' says Colette sarcastically.

'Oh my God,' shrieks her mother, rushing out of the room again, into her own bedroom. 'There's something else I've forgotten. I've got this book for you, a really exciting present . . .'

She rushes back and hands the book to Colette, still wrapped in its Waterstone's maroon-coloured carrier bag.

'No book can be exciting,' says Colette, ignoring the bag at first, till she has finished flicking through the magazine. Then she slowly opens it, watched carefully by her mother, who expects Colette's face to light up in appreciation.

'Oh, you stupid woman!' shouts Colette, hurling the book across the bedroom. 'I'm trying to forget it.

Take it back to the shop at once. I don't want it in this house at all.'

Her mother picks up the book, *Revision Guide to A Level French*. She looks at it, crestfallen.

'Get it out of my sight!' shrieks Colette. Her good humour has completely gone.

'But I had it recommended. Everyone says it's very good. You've been moaning so much about your French, so I thought anything that could help in some way must be useful.'

'But it can't! Don't you see? It's oral French I'm useless at, thanks to that stupid woman. This stupid book isn't going to help me with that, is it? Think about it. Oh God!'

'Sorry, darling.'

'Oh God,' says Colette, getting out of bed. 'Might as well go to school now.'

'Sorry,' says her mother again.

'Yes, I know you were only trying to help. But I've just made a vow not to think about French.'

'You haven't finished your soldiers,' says her mother plaintively.

'Bugger the soldiers,' says Colette. 'And get out of my bedroom.'

Taz: eager beaver

EPISODE 5

School, same day

It's lunchtime in the common room. Most people have already got their food from the canteen, or have brought their own, and are now sitting quietly, idly chatting, idly scoffing. Ella and Toby are at a table by the window, side by side. They are each working, writing furiously.

'Don't you feel out of it, you two?' asks Raffy.

'I beg your pardon?' says Ella, looking up from her book.

'I mean, there are two eager beavers going round, asking people dead serious questions, and neither of them are you.'

'Neither *is* you,' says Ella. 'It's singular.'

'I know, clever dick,' says Raffy. 'I did get an A in

54

GCSE English. But I'm talking, gerrit? Colloquial English, spoken English. Not the same as written English.'

'Good, I'm glad you realize,' says Ella, returning to her essay.

'Funny how we're always two people, in a way,' says Raffy. 'The way we talk, compared with the way we write. The accent we use at school, compared with the accent we use at home. The way we are nice to our friends, the way we are horrible to our parents. The way we act in our heads, the way we act in reality. The way we sound on tape, the way we sound in the flesh. The way we look in a photograph, the way we look in real life.'

'What is he on about?' asks Toby.

'Ignore him,' says Ella. 'Just hope he'll go away.'

'Which brings me to television,' continues Raffy. 'In this case, it disproves my rule. See above. Because on television – are you listening, Ella? – I'm gonna be huge, super, multi, extra, out of this world, just as I am in ordinary life. Right, can someone lend me a quid? I'm starving. Don't all rush.'

'Ah, Raffy,' says Dim, coming over with his notebook. 'I haven't asked you yet.'

'Lend us 50p first,' says Raffy, 'then I'm all yours. Up, down, how's your father, any way you like. Just give us the money.'

'It's only a random sample I'm doing,' says Dim, getting out fifty pence while looking at his notes. 'A cross section of the sixth form.'

'Yes, I'm going to vote Green at the next election,' says Raffy. 'Shoot them all, is what I say. Hanging's too good for them. No, I think water and electricity should not be nationalized. Yes, condoms should always be worn in bed. No, I can't tell Flora margarine from motor oil. Yes, I want all the Irish people out of Ireland, that's the only way. Yes, I think Mr Gorbachev should be the next Head Teacher of St Andrews Road School, if he isn't already, and Mrs Potter should leave for Russia, *toot de sweet . . .*'

Ella smiles, but stifles her smile quickly, before Raffy can see it. Dim was not listening properly. He started to write down these replies, thinking Raffy was answering the questions which he hadn't yet asked, and is now rubbing them out with his pencil.

'In an ideal world,' says Dim, clearing his throat, 'would you like something hot or cold at lunchtime?'

Even Toby smiles at this, before Raffy is able to make the obvious reply. Which does not, of course, stop him making it.

'Hot or cold what?' says Raffy. 'Women?'

'Food,' says Dim, without the trace of a smile.

'Ah, now you're talking. I thought it might be hot and cold running maids in every room. We could get them tonight, depending on where Jules says the big meeting is going to be. You are going, aren't you, Dim?'

'Maybe,' says Dim. 'I've got a lot to do. Look, don't muck around. Just answer simply, or I'll ask someone else.'

He turns to look at Toby, but Raffy drags him back.

'Don't ask him,' says Raffy. 'He's only been

in this school half an hour. Right, come on, I'm concentrating. Shoot.'

'What sort of sandwiches do you like best?'

'Thick ones,' says Raffy. Dim groans, but writes this down.

'What about drink?'

'Yes, put me down as a definite "yes". Social drinking only, of course. I made a rule years ago never to drink on the lavatory.'

Dim closes his notebook this time and walks away.

'I dunno,' says Raffy. 'He's got no sense of humour, that kid. Typical. Just like all scientists.'

'Perhaps he has,' says Ella, 'and you haven't.'

Another corner of the common room

Kirsty and Colette are sitting on the new couch together, their chosen venue. Ella, their normal partner, has decided she must work this break. Her place has been taken by Matt.

'Look, I'll draw it for you,' says Matt. 'Have you got any felt pens, coloured ones?'

'Oh Gawd,' says Kirsty. 'I lent mine to our Mandy and she's never returned them, rotten cow.'

'That's not a nice way to talk about your sister,' says Matt.

'Taz!' shouts Colette, seeing Taz working her way round the common room. She is the other person going round asking various people questions. 'Got any felt pens?'

'Sorry,' says Taz, coming over. 'Can I ask you all something?'

'Hold on a minute,' says Kirsty, 'Matt's in the middle of something.'

'Right,' says Matt, drawing with his finger on the new carpet, leaving little rutted marks. 'Just imagine a continent, any size you like, okay.'

'Sam,' shouts Colette. 'You do Geography, don't you? Come over here. You could learn something.'

'So do I, actually,' says Taz.

'Great,' says Matt, starting his map again. 'Right, let's say it's a map of the whole world if you like, which is full of countries, okay. One here, one there, all over the place, all different shapes. As many as you like. Okay?'

'Yes,' says Colette.

'Now this is really weird. To keep them all different, so that no two touching countries are the same colour, how many colours would you need to draw the whole map?'

'Ten?' asks Taz.

'Twelve?' asks Sam, running his fingers over the map.

'Nope,' says Matt.

'I give in,' says Kirsty. 'Tell me.'

'Only four,' says Matt triumphantly.

'So?' says Sam. 'Not very amazing.'

'Ah, but I'm now going to tell you something totally amazing. This will blow your mind, man. No one knows why.'

'How do you mean, no one knows?' says Kirsty. 'You've just told us. Four colours.'

'Yeah, but why, man? What's the explanation? Don't you see?'

'No,' says Sam.

'This fact was first observed in 1852, the so-called four-colour theorem, okay. But no mathematician, man, anywhere, has so far managed to write down a satisfactory explanation. Some Yankees recently did a sort of proof, but on a computer, yeah, and it took them 1,200 hours. So forget it, man. We're still waiting for the beautiful proof, the simple little explanation. Get my drift?'

'That's incredible,' says Kirsty.

'Gawd,' says Colette. 'I'm amazed.'

'Yes, that is most remarkable,' says Taz. 'But what I was going to ask you, all of you actually, is, well, you know it's the first staff meeting of term tomorrow, and I'm going, as you know. Well, I'm just asking a sample of people what I should bring up, if of course I can bring up anything.'

'French,' says Colette, quickly. 'I wanna know why it's so badly taught in this school.'

'Geography,' says Sam. 'Get rid of the whole department, and start again.'

'Hmm,' says Taz. 'I see. Well, I'll try my best. How about you, Matthew?'

'Maths,' says Matt. 'I fink it should be compulsory for everyone, right through the school. You know why?'

'No, do tell me,' says Taz.

'Cos it's beautiful.'

Fred's Caff, after school

There are only nine customers, sitting silently round a Formica-topped table, staring vacantly through the steamed-up windows. The mid-afternoon, late-lunch rush has long finished. So has the immediate post-school, hanging around rush. There will be a mini-rush around five, when local labourers grab some fried nourishment before the pubs start opening. But between four-thirty and five, things usually are pretty dead in Fred's Caff. The counter is emptied, the floor gets cleaned, tables sometimes wiped, as the end of another day is almost nigh.

The nine customers are obviously waiting for someone. Some sit expectantly, some impatiently, while three are simply bored. Raffy, Colette and Kirsty are amongst the expectant ones. All three have been home to change and freshen up, to look their best. Jules, the most expectant of all, thought out his wardrobe last night, and has taken care not to crease anything.

Taz and Dim are clearly impatient. They have been dragged along and want to be off as soon as possible, as they have better things to do. Sam, Ella and Toby are bored. They don't care, either way, about this TV show, whether it comes off or not.

Simon asked Jules to suggest a rendezvous, somewhere near school but not inside, as he has confidential matters to discuss. Fred's Caff was the first place Jules could think of. Now he is beginning to regret it. He hopes Simon will be here soon and whip them all off somewhere more salubrious.

'What I don't understand,' says Ella, 'is why you want to be famous, Raffy.'

'You trying to wind me up?' says Raffy, who is

drumming his fingers on the table. He jumps up to wipe the steam from the windows, then rushes to the counter for a paper napkin as he finds his fingers are filthy.

'No, seriously,' says Ella. 'I want to know.'

'In a word,' says Raffy, 'sex.'

'I thought as much,' says Ella.

'So why did you ask?' says Raffy. 'It's the number one motivation for the majority of people when they first begin, whether they're pop stars, politicians, footballers, or financiers. They think they'll pull more birds if they're rich and famous. And of course they do. It does work. They might not admit it, might use different words, but deep down the one thing they're all hoping to do is improve their sex appeal. Am I right or am I right?'

'How about you, Colette?' asks Toby.

'Power,' says Colette. 'When I'm famous, I'll be able to boss the whole world around.'

'You do already,' says Dim. 'Just ask your mum.'

'I mean it,' says Colette, giving Dim a push. 'I won't have to put up with shit and hassle from stupid teachers and stupid people. They'll be too busy keeping in with me.'

'How about you, Kirsty?' asks Toby.

'Freedom,' says Kirsty. 'Personal freedom. I don't want to boss anyone around, just to go off and do what I like, where I like, when I like.'

'Okay, fans, as we're going round the table,' says Jules. 'I'm in it for the fun, since you ask. I want to be recognized everywhere, pointed out in the playground, get the best table at Fred's, sign autographs for first-year kids. I want to bask in all the glory, so that everyone knows me, even better than they do now.'

'I think you are all living in a fantasy world,' says Taz. 'Fame is like wealth. Doesn't make you any happier. Doesn't change your personality. You're stuck with who you are. In fact, it can make you a worse person. It's also such a worry. Because you value it so much, you worry all the time about it going.'

They all listen quietly to Taz, for she rarely says so much. They all know she is the only one with wealth in her family, and are aware that it has led to problems for her father.

'Well, I don't really know about that,' says Ella, 'But it seems to me, Kirsty, you must lose freedom, not gain by it. Imagine being recognized all the time. Absolute strangers stopping and talking to you, as if they own a part of you. I'd hate that.'

'I can't wait,' says Raffy. 'In fact I'm getting pretty pissed off with waiting. Seventeen years and two months, and I'm still waiting. What time did he say, Jules?'

'Between four-thirty and five. He must have got stuck in the traffic at Shepherds Bush.'

'Where do you think he'll take us?' asks Kirsty, still all bright-eyed.

'Somewhere lovely, I hope,' says Jules.

The door opens and a scruffy, bearded man in an old parka comes in and goes to the counter. Fred, his usual welcoming self, grudgingly agrees to do ten teas plus two packets of the cheapest biscuits.

'Teas okay, Jules?' shouts the man. 'Or does anyone want coffee?'

'I didn't recognize you,' says Jules, jumping up. 'When did you grow the beard, Simon?'

'Oh, I have one every winter. My winter warmth. Saves on razor blades.'

Simon brings the teas across and sets them down. Jules, ever the gentleman, starts introducing the others one by one, but Simon is too busy trying to break into the Cellophane wrapping on the biscuits.

'Been editing all day. Not had a bite since breakfast. Anyone want one, hmm?'

When Simon has eaten almost all the biscuits, he pulls some notes out of a folder, the ones Jules sent him. He studies everyone in turn, checking the details, asking a few questions of each of them.

'I'm afraid this must be a quick meeting,' he says when he has gone round the table. 'It's just to say hello, as I'm afraid I've got to get back in about ten minutes. Haven't finished my present programme yet. It goes out on Monday evening, so I'm in the usual panic.'

'Which channel?' says Toby politely, making conversation.

'BBC 2, ten-thirty. You won't like it. Unemployment in West Cumbria. Frightfully dull. We had to do a studio discussion in the end as we couldn't get the right locations. That's why I'm so excited about this new programme. Jules has made your school sound really ace.'

'Well, it is,' says Raffy.

'Good. Well, I'll be in touch soon.'

Simon starts to get up, then pauses to finish off the last of the biscuits. 'Oh, one other thing. I'd better get down a list of your GCSE subjects, as I'd like to have a balance, science and arts.'

'We just have the usual ones,' says Jules. 'Seven or eight each, I think, like most people.'

'I thought it was only three? Well, it was in my day.'

'Actually, we all took eight,' says Raffy. 'Except, I think, Kirsty. We're all brain boxes except Kirsty. She's the sexpot.'

Kirsty gives Raffy a push, sending him sliding off his chair.

'You've *taken* them?' says Simon, sitting down again.

'That's right,' says Jules. 'Last year.'

'But I thought you were doing them now?'

'No,' says Toby slowly. 'You do GCSEs at sixteen, at the end of the fifth year. What used to be called O levels.'

'Yes, yes,' says Simon impatiently. 'I know that.'

'Then at eighteen,' continues Toby, 'in the upper sixth, you do three A levels.'

'But I thought that had changed as well. I thought it was all GCSE now, that A levels had gone as well as O levels.'

'No,' says Toby.

'So none of you are doing GCSE exams, at all?' Simon looks at his BBC issue folder, on the outside of which is the new programme's title, roughly done in Letraset: *Whither GCSE?*

'It was just a working title, of course,' he says mournfully. 'What a cock-up.'

'Is that it, then?' says Raffy. 'You don't want us any more?'

'No, no, I didn't say that,' says Simon, getting up. 'I think we can swing it. Not to worry. Look at the time, I must rush. Thanks for turning up, and thanks, Jules. Regards to your mother. I'll be in touch. Bye.'

Simon dashes out. Everyone at once turns on Jules.

'He's a complete idiot,' says Raffy.

'It'll obviously never happen now,' says Kirsty sadly.

'And we didn't even get a free meal out of it,' says Colette, as they all get up to leave.

'Don't get too depressed,' says Jules, but with little conviction. 'I'm sure something will come of it.'

'It has,' says Taz. She has noticed that Fred is waving at them from behind the counter. He then rushes over and pushes something into Taz's hand.

'We've got a bill for ten teas and two packets of biscuits.'

'Oh Gawd,' says Raffy. 'The rotten sod.'

'Don't worry,' says Taz. 'I'll pay. I might not be famous, but I have got money.'

Dim: full of vim

EPISODE 6

One week later. School, tutor room.

There is an air of quiet resignation as another week begins. January has gone on too long, like a rubber month, stretching itself, the end moving away rather than coming nearer. The excitement which had been hoped for, a little bit of action in a dreadfully dull month, has not materialized. Jules has not heard from Simon. All the stars-to-be now feel more deflated than they were before the idea had ever been trailed in front of them.

Only Dim is full of vim, and a bit of vigour, but then he had no interest in appearing on TV. Taz is low as well, not because of the documentary, as she had no interest in it either, but because her appearance at the staff meeting turned out to be less than wonderful.

'So what happened?' asks Ella.

'Nothing, really,' replies Taz. 'I was sent outside when they discussed one item, about whether some new teacher would get a scale post or not, as it could have become confidential. Mainly, they went on and on about the National Curriculum. All complaining about the extra work it would cause them.'

'Did you speak?' asks Toby.

'No, that was the worst of all. I hadn't realized that I'm only there as an observer. I only get to talk if someone asks my view, which they didn't.'

'Rotten lot,' says Ella. 'Not even on the National Curriculum?'

'Nope,' says Taz.

'We've been conned,' says Toby.

'We should never have trusted Mrs Potter,' says Ella. 'She gave in far too easily. We should have realized what would happen.'

'I think she's a good bloke,' says Dim. 'Have you heard? She's agreed to me taking on the sixth-form tuckshop.'

'How very exciting,' says Ella. 'But what good does that do?'

'A lot,' says Dim. 'I've got a rota of ten people who will serve during free periods. I'm giving a percentage of all profits to the Sixth-Form Fund. I'm doing things, Ella, not just talking things, see.'

'That is true,' says Toby, using Ella's favourite phrase.

'And it's only the beginning,' says Dim. 'This term, St Andrews. Next term, London. After that, the nation. Once I've sussed it all out, we'll have a chain of tuckshops, coast to coast, in every sixth form in the land. Then we'll move back, economically speaking, to the means of supply. We'll have sixth-form own brand goods, which we'll manufacture. I estimate there's almost a million sixth formers, and the numbers are growing all the time. Most people don't leave school at sixteen now, but stay on. I've worked it all out. Properly organized, we could have enormous financial and economic power, all starting from our little tuckshop.'

Dim stands back, out of breath with his long speech, carried away by his own excitement. For a moment, Toby, Ella and Taz are lost for words. Into the little gap of silence slides Matt.

'Isn't Mathematics wonderful?' he says, pulling aside his hair and smiling like a cherub. 'Did you have a chance, Taz, to bring it up at the staff meeting, what I said to you?'

'Very sorry, Matthew, I just didn't manage to work it in.'

'Oh, not to worry,' says Matt, sweetly. 'Another time. By the way, do you know why our numbers system is based on tens? You know, why we count in tens? We go one to ten, don't we, then on to twenty, and so on, the decimal system.'

'Tell me,' says Taz.

'Because we have ten fingers?' asks Ella.

'You've got it,' says Matt. 'But if we'd had, say, twenty-six fingers on our hands, and counted in twenty-sixes, the primes would still be the same. Isn't that amazing?'

'I suppose so,' says Ella, trying to remember what a prime is.

'The Babylonians based their numbers on a sixty system,' says Matt.

'Did they have sixty fingers?' asks Sam.

'No,' says Matt, laughing. 'Actually, I don't know why they chose sixty. I'll have to find out. But we inherited part of their system, for counting time.'

'You mean in the boozer at the end of the evening?' says Sam. He is becoming a bit fed-up about the way Ella, and the other girls, always seem to find Matt so fascinating.

'No, I mean for measuring time, which we still do in sixties, not in tens. We have sixty seconds in a minute, don't we, and sixty minutes in an hour. And it all comes from how they used to count in Babylon. You've got to admit it. Isn't Maths –'

' – beautiful,' say Ella, Kirsty and Colette as one, singing in chorus. They all burst out laughing, till Mr Grott bangs on his desk and calls for silence.

'Before you all go off for the day's excitements, I've had an urgent message from Mrs Potter. There are two people she wants to see urgently at break-time.'

The girls stop laughing. People stand still in front of their lockers, listening.

'Now hold on, where have I put their names? Anybody seen that message Mrs Buttock brought in?'

Dim immediately thinks the message must be for

him. Mrs Potter, perhaps, wants him to go nation-
wide at once. Matt imagines it could be for him. His
campaign for Maths is about to get off the ground.
Raffy thinks it might concern him, as anyone in their
right mind would naturally want to see him, about
anything, at any time. Sam half fears it might be
about his Geography. His father has said he would
write to the school, which Sam now thinks would be
a big mistake. Colette half hopes it might be the
result of the scene she caused in the last French oral
test, asking for the teacher to be sacked.

'Ah, here it is,' says Mr Grott. 'Jules and, let me
see, Taz. Yes, the two of you are wanted by Mrs
Potter. Eleven o'clock prompt.'

Outside the Head's office, eleven o'clock

Taz and Jules are sitting in the outer office, listening
to the clatter and chatter through the open door
where Mrs Buttock and the other school secretaries
are working away. Both of them are looking straight
ahead, watching Mrs Potter's door, which is firmly
closed. They keep an eye on her traffic lights,
waiting for them to turn green, the sign for them to
enter.

Neither can work out why they have been called
to the presence, nor why they have to go in together.
That's what Mrs Buttock has told them to do. Same
tutor group, that's true. Quite good friends now,
also true, but not long-established ones, as Taz is
still fairly new to the school. So what can the
connection be?

They can hear a female voice in the secretaries'

office. Some parent has burst in and is now apologizing, saying no, she hasn't got an appointment, but she's come from work, especially, in the hope of seeing Mrs Potter about an urgent matter. She'll wait, and just take her chance.

'Oh hello, Mrs Cavendish,' says Jules, when the woman comes in. It is Colette's mother.

'Jules, how lovely to see you. So I have come to the right place. I was worried it wasn't even the right school. It's just so enormous. I don't know how you all cope.'

'This is Taz,' says Jules. 'She's in our tutor group.'

'Of course, I've heard all about you.'

The traffic lights turn green. Jules jumps up at once, waiting for someone to come out, but no one does. Colette's mother looks confused. So does Taz, not being used to the system. Jules stops, wondering what to do.

'Go in!' shouts Mrs Buttock from the other office. 'Hurry up. There is a queue, you know.'

Colette's mother, Jules and Taz all move for the door at once, banging into each other, then they all apologize. Colette's mother sits down again, saying she'll wait as she hasn't got an appointment. She is beginning to look rather nervous. What if Colette has been spinning her stories, imagining that the French lessons are so bad, or just exaggerating, to cover her own inadequacies?

Jules and Taz knock, and go straight in.

Inside Mrs Potter's office

Mrs Potter is at her desk, looking very executive. Opposite, on her couch, sits Simon, looking rather smug, along with a young, trendily dressed woman aged about twenty-five.

'Simon!' says Jules, coming into the room with Taz. 'I didn't know you were here.'

'We've just been having a very fruitful meeting,' says Simon. 'But I'd better let your Head Mistress explain everything.'

'Head Teacher, please,' says Mrs Potter.

'Sorry,' says Simon. 'I keep showing my ignorance. Schools have changed so much in the fifteen years since I left. That's why I'm looking forward to making this film so much. I can see I'm going to learn a lot myself. Oh, by the way, this is Binky. She'll be researching the programme. This is Taz and this is Jules.'

'Right,' says Mrs Potter, when all the introductions have been made. 'I gather you know a little bit about this proposed television documentary, Jules? I understand you were instrumental in bringing Simon to the school.'

'That's right,' says Jules, smiling, feeling pleased with himself.

'Not quite right,' says Simon, quickly sensing a possible political slight. 'As you know, I'd met Jules during his work shadowing, so when I was looking for a sixth former, I naturally contacted him, amongst others. But our first chat was purely informal, before, of course, making an official approach to you, Mrs Potter.'

'Thank you,' says Mrs Potter. 'Well, this morning I have cleared the matter with my Chairman of Governors and senior staff. We are prepared to give you full facilities for the programme you have out-lined, about our sixth form.'

Jules is watching Simon carefully as he smarms over Mrs Potter, charming her, or so he thinks. He is beginning to decide Simon is a bit creepy. And he's also getting worried about Mrs Potter's possi-ble role in all this. Her talk of 'our sixth form' is rather suspicious, when Jules has been promised he will be the presenter of what he is determined to turn into his show.

'Oh, Mrs Potter, that's absolutely smashing of you,' says Simon, fawning even more. 'And I'm grateful to you for suggesting such a strong theme. Aren't we, Binky?'

'Yeah,' says Binky, crossing her long and elegant legs.

'I did point out to the Head of Features,' says Simon, 'that it was really rather silly to go on about GCSE in a sixth-form programme, har har. That was his original idea, har har.'

'But there is one condition,' says Mrs Potter.

Simon immediately looks worried. Binky ceases her Sloaney smiling.

'We do not want to censor you in any way,' continues Mrs Potter. 'We realize you have your job to do, and you must shoot as you see fit. And we naturally trust the BBC to produce a fair and balanced film.'

'Oh, we'll certainly try to,' says Simon quickly.

'What I am insisting, is that two people from the school will have the opportunity to see the finished film before it goes out, purely to correct any inaccuracies.'

'Oh, I'm afraid that is not really possible,' says Simon. 'You see it's not our policy –'

'In that case,' says Mrs Potter, 'the deal is off.'

'What?' says Simon.

'We are living in very sensitive times. Not just because of various Government policies and changes about to be implemented, but because the whole of the comprehensive system has been treated badly by the media at large. I'm not accusing you at the BBC, but in general we have been prejudiced against.'

There is a long pause. Mrs Potter looks adamant. Simon and Binky exchange worried looks.

'Tell you what, Mrs Potter,' says Binky. 'I have a suggestion. I'm sure it would be possible for just you, alone, to have a screening of the rough cut. Okay, Simon?'

Simon looks a bit wary.

'You see,' says Binky, 'if we wait to the end and we *have* got anything wrong, which I'm absolutely sure we won't have, it will be too expensive to change. After the rough cut, nothing else will be put in, just polishing really, editing. So I'm sure you could see that, and we could alter any factual mistakes then. Hmm?'

'We would accept that,' says Mrs Potter.

'But I don't want lots of people looking at it,' says

Simon. 'You know what it's like. They'll all have different opinions.'

'I was thinking of only two people,' says Mrs Potter. 'Myself, as Head, and Taz, as a sixth former. That's why I've asked her to be here. She happens to be the sixth form's rep at staff meetings. So, does that seem fair?'

Simon still looks worried, but nods. They all shake hands.

'Good,' says Mrs Potter, as they all start to leave. 'And I gather you are going to be the real star, Jules.'

Jules smiles, trying to look casual. 'That's what my agent tells me,' he says.

'We won't be having a presenter, in the normal sense,' says Simon hurriedly. 'My plan at the moment is to start by having a sixth former, such as Jules, showing us round the school.'

'Sounds a jolly good idea,' says Mrs Potter. Jules beams.

'But the plan could change,' says Simon, 'now that you have suggested such an excellent theme.'

Jules stops smiling. On Binky's clipboard, he has noticed a new title for the programme: *Whither the National Curriculum?*

Later that evening, Marine Ices restaurant

All nine of them, television stars-to-be, are tucking into a lavish Italian meal and a great deal of Italian wine. Their hosts are Simon and Binky.

'Gawd, it was awful of me not to have paid for those teas,' says Simon. 'Will you ever forgive me?'

'We just thought it was typical BBC,' says Raffy. 'Too mean.'

'I will have to work hard to swing this on expenses,' says Simon.

'So I can't have some more wine then?' says Raffy.

'Of course you can, silly boy,' says Binky, calling over a waiter and ordering more drinks all round, except for Taz, who does not drink.

The party is getting rather noisy, especially Raffy's side of it. He is sitting beside Binky, convinced he is making a great impression. She has laughed at all his jokes. In fact, at everyone's jokes.

'Tell me more about yourself, Raffy,' says Binky, moving closer to him, not wanting to miss any pearls.

'Well, I can let you see pictures if you like,' says Raffy. 'Or etchings. But you'll have to see them in my bedroom, okay yeah? Get my drift?'

'And why not?' says Binky. 'We might be doing some location work in people's homes. Could we film in your bedroom, then?'

Raffy explains it was just a joke, not wanting anyone to see his room. 'But I can come round to *your* bedroom any time,' he says.

'Super,' says Binky. 'Tell me, what are your other interests, apart from trying to get into strange girls' bedrooms?'

'Well, that takes up a lot of time,' says Raffy. 'I've got quite a few to get round.'

'Anything else?' says Binky. 'Hobbies, I mean, outside interests?'

'I follow football,' says Raffy.

'No, he doesn't,' says Sam. 'He follows Arsenal.'

'Shut up, you,' says Raffy, pushing Sam away. 'She's asking me, rot guts, so keep out of it. Aren't you, darling?'

'I sure am,' says Binky. She has now produced a pad and is ready to make notes, sitting poised in front of a blank sheet which has Raffy's name at the top. Raffy suddenly realizes that this is for real, and he's not doing very well. He has always been convinced that he is the wittiest, smartest, cleverest person in the whole Sixth, but he is beginning to wonder whether this information is somehow not getting across to Binky.

'Right, what about you, Sam?' says Binky, abruptly turning her back on Raffy.

Sam can't think of much either. Nor can most of the others when Binky, moving around the table, talks to each of them in turn. Apart from Dim. By chance, Binky gets him going on the tuckshop, and his big plans for the future.

'Boring, boring,' shouts Raffy down the table. 'You want to talk to me, me, me. He's a scientist. Boring, boring.'

Raffy has had a little too much to drink by now, so Taz takes away his glass when he's not watching.

'What's this new theme, Simon, which Mrs Potter has suggested?' asks Taz.

'*Whither the National Curriculum?*' interrupts Jules. 'Sounds very draggy.'

'"Whither" is just a joke,' says Simon. 'My secretary always puts it on the sheets at this stage. We'll find a better title by the time we've finished.'

'I don't even know what it means,' says Jules.

'I don't either,' says Simon. 'But don't tell any-one.'

'I know all about it,' says Taz. 'The staff are in absolute panic stations. It's all they talk about.'

'The subject isn't really too vital,' says Simon. 'What happens is that we have to do one educational programme in our thirteen-week run, and I wanted to shoot in a comprehensive sixth form. I thought it would be fun.'

'So that's the way it works,' says Ella. 'You don't really care?'

'I didn't say that,' says Simon.

'I think you've been conned by Mrs Potter,' says Jules. 'She and the staff just want to get in on this film, to put across their boring views on the National Curriculum. We haven't even been told about it yet.'

'There's one thing you could do,' says Taz, 'that would be new. Get *our* views on the new curriculum. After all, we are going to be the consumers. It affects us more than the staff.'

'Hey, that's a terrific idea,' says Simon. 'Get that down, Binky.'

'You could look at what we do today,' says Ella. 'Our present curriculum, lessons as well as all the other activities, then at how things will change when the new curriculum comes in.'

'Fantastic,' says Simon. 'Did you hear that as well, Binky?'

'Yes, Binky,' says Raffy, leaning over the table

and trying to grab her, while she talks to Dim. 'Get 'em all down, Binky.'

Everyone laughs. Except Jules. He has a new worry. First it was the staff trying to take over his programme. Now it's the girls, Taz and Ella, suggesting their own ideas. The sooner they start shooting his film the better.

Sam: hates everybody

EPISODE 7

One week later, Jules's flat,
after school

Jules is pressing the intercom on the front door of his flat, as he has done for years, every time he arrives home.

'Hi there, Jules,' he says, speaking into it. 'It's me, Jules. Home again, home again, jiggety jig.'

At the same time, he opens the door with his keys, the Ingersoll and the Chubb, and walks in, humming to himself.

'One of these years there's bound to be a reply,' he thinks. 'And I'll jump right out of my skin.'

It's all part of Jules's coming-home ritual, banishing the daytime spirits which have been languishing in the empty flat. For over five years, since he started at St Andrews, he has been a latch-key kid, coming home after school each day to

80

an empty flat. In the early days, the rituals were to give himself reassurance, stop him from being scared there might be burglars inside. Now he does it without thinking.

Jules is feeling pretty pleased with himself, though rather tired. Today has been the first day of shooting. The cameras have been in school all day, mainly following him around.

'Hello there, Jules,' he says to himself in the hall mirror, checking out the old face, another of his coming-home routines. 'Nice to see you. Had a good day, hmm? God, I hope they got my best side in that last shot.'

He then goes down the corridor, knocking on his bedroom door with the palm of his hand, without going in. Yet another old habit, re-establishing his territory. He goes into the kitchen and takes a bottle of Perrier out of the fridge, pours the contents into a glass, then adds ice and lemon.

'Oh, so nice to be home. I don't know how they manage on a big shoot, on the set day after day, performing all the time. I think performing to the crew is more tiring than performing to the camera.'

He takes his shoes off, turns on the stereo, choosing a piece of classic Courtney Pine, then flops down on the best couch, cuddling a cushion to himself. His mother hates him doing this, as she says it makes him look retarded. On your own, you can do what you like. He picks up the *Radio Times*, to see what's on television tonight, then flicks back to the front cover.

'I wonder if we'll make it to the cover. And should

I wear shades or not? Goodness, so many things still to be decided.'

The phone rings. Jules starts to get up to answer, then pauses, thinks, frowns. He waits till it stops ringing, then stands up and dials a number.

'Hello? Oh, hello. It's Jules here . . . You know, from school. *That* Jules. Anyway, is Matt at home? . . . Yes Matt, Matthew. You know? . . . Could you ask him to ring me then? Later tonight, if he does get home tonight. Thanks.'

Jules hangs up, then dictates a message into the answering machine. 'This is Jules speaking, star of stage, screen and St Andrews sixth-form common room. Awfully sorry, but I've had to go out. Yes, another audition, what a bore. ITV is after me this time. So I won't be in for a while. But if you want to leave a message, please speak slowly after the peeps. My butler will probably ring you back, some time . . .'

Meanwhile, at Sam's house

Sam is standing on his front doorstep, fighting and pushing, cursing and swearing, beginning to lose a battle which has gone on for the last five minutes. A minor skirmish in a war which first began fifteen years ago. Sarah, his younger sister, aged fifteen, kicks away Sam's plastic carrier bag. While he stoops to pick it up, she gets the front door open and bounds down the hall.

'You pig,' shouts Sam after her.

'Mum!' shouts Sarah. 'Sam has been horrible to me.'

There is no reply, which is unusual. Their mother has a part-time job, and is usually at home for their arrival back from school.

Sam follows Sarah into the kitchen, where she's standing reading a note.

'Oh God, she's not in,' says Sam. 'Stupid woman.'

'It says you've got to go and do some shopping.'

'Get lost,' says Sam. 'You read it first. *You* do the shopping.'

'But she's left something for us in the fridge,' reads Sarah.

Sam dashes to the fridge, gets there first, and pulls out a plate with two slices of cheesecake on it. He proceeds to ram both slices down his mouth, keeping Sarah away with his foot.

'Gerroff,' says Sarah. 'One of those is for me.'

'Too late,' says Sam, swallowing the last mouthful. 'Serves you right.'

'You are so mean,' says Sarah, hitting him. 'And stupid. You'll just get spots. Even more than you have already.'

'Don't care,' says Sam. 'Don't care if my whole face is full of spots. Not now.'

'You're doing the shopping, anyway,' says Sarah, opening a cupboard, looking for something, anything, to eat.

'I feel sick,' says Sam. 'I shouldn't have eaten two pieces.'

'Good, I'm pleased,' says Sarah.

'But I needed them. I've had a really awful day and I'm really fed-up and I hate everybody.'

'Oh, shurrup,' says Sarah. 'Stop moaning on. Save it all for Mum. She's stupid enough to listen to you.'

'Please go to the shop, Sarah,' says Sam. 'Really, I'm knackered. Got the most splitting headache. Had it all day.'

'Not my fault,' says Sarah.

'Didn't say it was,' says Sam. 'Just today was so depressing.'

'Today?' says Sarah, still looking for something to eat. 'What was today? Oh, your potty little TV thing. Didn't they turn up, or something? Never saw them at school.'

'They were in our common room, all day.'

'That must have been interesting.'

'No it wasn't,' says Sam. 'They didn't use me.'

'Don't blame them,' says Sarah. 'I wouldn't use you either. You're just a moan.'

'Thanks, Sarah,' says Sam, looking very depressed.

'Okay, I will go,' says Sarah. 'On one condition. That you don't talk or make any clever remarks during *Neighbours*. Okay?'

'Don't worry,' says Sam. 'I'm not going to watch it tonight. I hate all television . . . and all television people.'

Kirsty's flat, meanwhile

Kirsty is slumped in a chair, flicking through the *Evening Standard*, looking for her horoscope.

'Are you sure, Kirsten?' asks her mother. She is

setting the table, ready for the workers coming home.

'Look, don't go on about it,' says Kirsty. 'I told you.'

'You're not sickening for something, are you?'

'No, I just don't feel hungry.'

'You been feeding your face at school?'

'What with? You know I haven't got any money.'

'Well, something's happened at school today, to make you so grumpy.'

'Nothing happened at school today,' says Kirsty. 'That's the problem.'

'What did you say, dear?'

'Nothing, nothing,' says Kirsty.

She has deliberately not told her mother that today was the first day of shooting. She decided a week ago to keep it quiet, to stop her mother telling any more of the neighbours about the programme. Just as well, the way things have turned out.

The flat door opens and in comes Kevin, filthy all over, soil and dust falling from his clothes. He comes into the living room, dropping dirt everywhere, and starts to unzip his boilersuit.

'Must you do that in here?' shouts Kirsty at him. 'Mum just has to clear up your mess.'

'So?' says Kevin. 'You don't have to do it. Just keep your big nose out of it, eh?'

'Pig,' says Kirsty.

'Some of us work for a living, and bring money into this place,' says Kevin. 'Unlike other people.'

'Get lost,' says Kirsty.

'Now, now, you two,' says their mother.

'She is in a bad mood,' says Kevin. 'Aren't you going to be a superstar then, after all?'

Kirsty holds up the newspaper so she can't see him, pretending to read her stars.

'Oh, lost her tongue now, has she? That won't do on the telly, will it? You'll have to chatter away then, won't you?'

'Leave her alone, Kevin,' says their mother. 'She's not feeling well. I think she's sickening.'

'I'm feeling perfectly well!' shouts Kirsty. 'Just leave me alone.'

'So what happened, then?' says Kevin.

Kirsty ignores him. Their mother makes a face, warning Kevin to leave her alone.

'I passed your school today. Saw this BBC car going in. Loada stuff they had. How did it go then, Kirst? Were you good, eh?'

'Oh God, there's no privacy at all in this place,' says Kirsty, jumping up and throwing the paper on the floor. 'I'm going to bed.'

'At this time?' says her mother. 'Oh, Kirsty. Shall I bring you some soup?'

'Leave her alone,' says Kevin. He picks up the newspaper and turns to the horoscope pages. 'What's Kirsty? Virgo, is she? Some chance. They're all rubbish anyway. I dunno why she takes such notice of them. When's her birthday, Mum?'

'October the first. You know that, Kevin.'

'Oh yeah, Libra. Listen to this: "For reasons best known to yourself, you appear to be almost desperate for a change of scenery or even a new lifestyle. However, loved ones are also eager for you to be more interested in what is taking place on the home front and require certain assurances."

'Hey, that's bloody good. Spot on.'

Colette's home, later the same evening

Colette and her mother have just finished their evening meal.

'Well, it's lucky the common room has just been finished,' says her mother, clearing the table.

'I don't see why,' says Colette, going to a chair and pulling up the cushions.

'It will look so much better in the programme. You've told me yourself that it was always so scruffy. It will be a good advert for state schools.'

'I don't give a damn about that. You're as bad as Mrs Potter, turning it all into PR for the school.'

'That is rather better, don't you think, than wanting to turn it into PR for yourself.'

'What do you mean by that?' says Colette. 'I hope you don't mean me? I wanted to be in it because, well, I wanted to be in it. I was promised I would be in it by that Jules. What a pig he is! He's the one who's on an ego trip.'

'Now don't say that,' says her mother. 'I'm sure it wasn't his fault.'

'Oh God, whose side are you on?' says Colette. She has now moved to the couch and is throwing cushions all over the floor.

'What are you looking for?' asks her mother.

'Nothing,' says Colette. 'Anyway, it's going to be a really boring programme. Glad I'm not going to be in it. Stupid new curriculum. Who cares about that? They'll all turn off at once.'

'Well, I'm looking forward to it,' says her mother. 'I think it's very interesting. I thought you would be interested, too. French is going to be given a better deal. You won't be able to drop it at fourteen, the way you used to. Everyone will have to do one foreign language, up to sixteen. We're already 5,000 language teachers short as it is, so they'll have to do something. Mrs Potter says it will make a big difference.'

'Who told you that? Have you been speaking to Mrs Potter?'

'Er, I think I read it in one of the Bulletins, weeks ago,' says her mother quickly.

'I never read them. Loada rubbish.'

'What on earth are you looking for, child?'

'I left some chocolate on this chair last night, under this cushion, and *someone* has stolen it. It must be you.'

'Oh, Colette. How can you eat chocolate, after that lovely meal?'

'Easy, just open my gob, and shove it down. Takes no cleverness, you don't need A levels, and yes, I know, it is very stupid, though not quite as stupid as smoking cigarettes all day long, like you.'

'Well, just think back,' says her mother, looking round all the chairs. 'Where did you leave it? I honestly didn't take it.'

'I want it *now*,' shrieks Colette. 'I need it. I'm just so depressed.'

'Now that is silly,' says her mother. 'You're being

melodramatic. They couldn't have everyone in this programme, could they? Stands to reason.'

'They said they would. They promised they would. Come on then, why did that sod Simon and that bitch Binky take all nine of us out to dinner?'

'Yes, dear, but that was before they decided to use the staff, and feature the National Curriculum.'

'You are so *stupid*. They already knew that. Our meal was afterwards. They lied to us, that's what. Saying they wanted the nine of us, getting us all excited, then when they start the bloody shooting, turns out they only need four of us. So humiliating. I probably won't go into school tomorrow.'

'Now that would be petty.'

'Good.'

'You might have told me, but tell me again, dear, who is in?'

'God, I've told you. Only four. Two girls, and two boys.'

'That sounds reasonable.'

'Is it, hell. Okay, Jules began it all, but choosing Dim is ridiculous. He can't string two words together. Just because of his stupid tuckshop.'

'Well that makes sense to me. I can see they'd want people who are doing things, something they can film.'

'Oh shut up, you don't know anything.'

'And Jules is a good talker.'

'So is Raffy,' says Colette. 'Far better than Dim. Raffy's absolutely furious. He's been ringing Jules all night, but Jules is hiding. Raffy says he's going to thump him.'

'And who are the girls?'

'Oh God, you never listen. I told you. Taz and Ella.'

'Oh, well. Taz is lovely-looking, and she wears super clothes, so you say.'

Colette picks up a cushion and throws it at her mother. 'I never thought I'd hear you come out with such sexist rubbish.'

'I'm only putting myself in their shoes. I'm sure that's how the television people decided.'

'Just give over, Mother,' says Colette.

'Taz is also on the Sixth-Form Council or something, isn't she? Hasn't she suddenly become an activist? Ella always has been. So there you are. They can film them in their meetings, or whatever.

'As for Sam and Raffy and you and Kirsty, well, you don't exactly join things, or do things for the school, do you, Colette?'

'What about Toby?' snarls Colette.

'Yes, but he's new to the school.'

'So is Taz!' says Colette triumphantly. 'So sussed. You think you're so clever, but you don't know what the hell you're talking about.'

Colette's mother goes to their old and battered welsh dresser and opens the first drawer, their so-called paper drawer, which is jammed with plastic carriers, paper bags, string and assorted rubbish. She pulls it open with a struggle, and from the back takes out a Marathon bar, rather faded, rather sticky.

'I was keeping this for emergencies,' she says, throwing it to Colette, who scoffs it straight away.

'Thanks, Mum.'

'Though really, Colette. This has all got out of proportion. It's only a television programme. You'll have far more worrying things in your life to get upset about than that.'

'Sorry, Mum,' says Colette. 'Any more chocolate?'

Jules: pure gold-dust

EPISODE 8

Sixth-form common room,
Friday lunchtime

It's nearing the end of the week, and also the end of the television filming. Most sixth formers have become so used to seeing the TV crew in the school that they just ignore it now, getting on with their own concerns: reading, eating, chattering. A few, though, are still gaping. Notably Raffy.

The TV people are working in a far corner of the common room, near the glass door into the little garden-cum-yard. They are shooting on video, so each evening they have had a run-through of the day's material in the library, for the crew to spot any technical faults, and for the stars, such as Jules, to see themselves. He has reported back, to those willing to listen, that so far he has been magic, pure gold-dust.

'So what's this bit, then, Si?' says Raffy, hanging about, getting in the way as the camera is being set up, the cables laid, the lights positioned, and the sound tested. There are seven in the crew altogether: a cameraman and his assistant, a sound engineer, an electrician, who has done very little all week, plus Simon the director, Binky the researcher, and Joyce the PA, or production assistant, who has a stop-watch and clipboard and keeps a note of all the shots.

'Just a little scene,' says Simon. 'The beginning bit, where Jules shows us round the common room.'

'Didn't you do that on the first day?' says Raffy.

'Yes,' says Simon, 'but it wasn't quite right.'

'You mean Jules wasn't quite right,' says Raffy.

'Well, he has got better as the week has gone on,' says Simon.

'Ah ha,' says Raffy, shouting through the open door. 'You made a mess of this scene first time, didn't you, Jules?'

Jules can't hear. He is in the garden, mouthing the words he is about to say and looking at his reflection in the glass door.

'He's done jolly well,' says Binky.

'Huh, anybody can do what he's done,' says Raffy.

'You'd be surprised how many people can't,' says Binky. 'There's a lot to remember, while trying to be natural at the same time.'

'Jules has never been natural,' says Raffy.

'Perhaps that's his secret,' says Simon. 'Anyway, if you could just stand over there, Raffy, please. We're about to begin.'

'What shots are we doing this afternoon, Simon?' asks Joyce. 'When we've done this, I think we've only got the front gates to do again. Then what? We've got the crew till four.'

'Hmm, I've been thinking about that,' says Simon. 'We could use another sixth former. If this goes well, and we get it done quickly. We'll see. Ready out there, Jules?'

Raffy has been listening hard. He looks around, to make sure none of the others has heard. Colette, Kirsty, Toby and Sam are right across the common room, by the couch, refusing to watch the filming, trying hard to rise above it, showing they are not interested in such trivial pursuits. Raffy, however, has no such pride.

Around the couch, at the other end of the common room

Matt arrives and sits down on the couch, between Kirsty and Colette. He pulls out a copy of *Kerrang!* and begins reading it. Kirsty and Colette make faces at each other, then return to their food and their chat.

'I don't understand that magazine,' says Toby. 'It seems to be written in a foreign language. Mind you, I don't understand the attraction of Heavy Metal anyway.'

'Matt,' says Kirsty, giving Matt a shove. 'You're being got at.'

'What's that, man?' says Matt. 'Didn't hear you.'

'He's going deaf now,' says Colette. 'From all that loud music.'

'I have got a headache today,' says Matt.

'And all that head-banging,' says Kirsty.

'That's out, man,' says Matt. 'What you do now is slamming, or windmilling, when you put your head like this . . .'

'Stop it,' says Colette. 'You're shaking the whole couch.'

'Sorry,' says Matt.

'It's so violent,' says Toby, looking at Matt's magazine over his shoulder. 'All this death stuff. And the names are so horrible, just like those horror movies you seem to love.'

'Well, Matt isn't horrible. Are you, Matt?' says Colette. 'All he does is sit around and drink beer and then fall asleep.'

'That's when he's not doing his Maths,' says Kirsty.

'Concerts, man,' says Matt. 'Don't forget them. Last weekend, right, I went to Paris for this gig. There were 10,000 of us there, right, and not one arrest, no violence, no trouble, nuffink.'

'That's cos you were all stoned,' says Kirsty. 'Or too deaf.'

'No, we only drink beer, man. It's cos of the music. It's so fast and loud. Takes all your aggression away. That's why it's so –'

'Beautiful?' says Kirsty, smiling at Colette.

'Right,' says Matt.

'Tell you what, take me next time,' says Colette. 'I need all the help with French I can get.'

'And me,' says Sam. 'I'm doing Paris for Urban Geography.'

'Right,' says Matt, then he seems to fall asleep.

Back on location, across at the other side of the common room

'Ready when you are, Jules,' shouts Simon.

'What about "Action"?' whispers Raffy. 'You've forgotten to say it.'

'Shush,' says Binky.

'I dunno,' says Raffy. 'I could do this programme better than any of you lot. Appearing *and* directing. Bunch of amateurs, if you ask me.' Raffy has been in films for years, all of them made in his own head. He follows himself around, and in these self-made, hand-held films, he's always shouted 'Action' and 'Cut'.

Jules comes from behind a tree, walks across the little garden, and at a point marked on the ground with a broken stick, invisible to any viewer, he starts talking.

'We don't have any smoking in our common room,' says Jules. 'It was our democratic decision to ban it, not because of any school rules. But out here in the garden is the place where smokers usually go, if they're stupid enough to want to smoke . . .'

He keeps on walking, going through the open glass door into the common room, turns left at a chalk mark on the carpet, as directed, then looks towards the camera, about to speak again.

'Stop,' says the cameraman. 'I'm getting reflections on the door. You can see a figure watching Justin.'

'Jules,' says Binky. Then, under her breath, 'For the fifteenth time.'

Simon looks around, trying to work out why there should be reflections, and sees that Raffy has ventured forward, getting himself in the shot. Joyce pushes Raffy back, warning him that he will have to leave the area unless he stands well away.

Jules is sent back to the tree, and everything starts again.

'We don't have any smoking in our common room,' he begins. 'It was our democratic –'

'Stop,' says the sound engineer, taking off his head phones. He puts them down dramatically, as if something really awful has happened. 'It's that bloody helicopter again,' he says. 'I'm picking it up.'

'In our common room?' says Raffy. 'Never noticed one before. I know people come by car these days, but not helicopter. Unless it's my friend Taz, she's loaded.'

'Shush,' says Joyce to Raffy.

Simon goes across to the sound man and listens to his machine.

'What an old woman he is,' says Binky softly.

'Don't worry too much,' says Simon. 'Just give it a minute. I think it's a traffic spotter, going round and round. We can always take a shot of it later, if we pick it up again. Okay, Jules? Ready when you are, sunshine.'

Jules returns to his tree, finds his mark, smiles, coughs, clears his throat, then starts again.

'In our common room –'

'Stop,' says Joyce. 'Continuity.'

'Oh, what the hell is it now?' says Simon, very bad-temperedly.

Joyce is quickly going through a pile of her notes, looking for something.

'I don't think he was wearing those sun-specs when we first saw him,' says Joyce. She and Simon go into a confab together.

'Where we going for lunch, Binks?' says the assistant cameraman, sitting on the camera-box and yawning.

'I'm not sure,' says Binky, giving her charming smile. 'Somewhere lovely.'

'It had better be. I'm not going to that caff again.'

'I know a good Indian down Camden Town,' says the sound man. 'Near the tube.'

'Not that one,' says the cameraman. 'I fancy that Chinese in Hampstead. Zen Something. Looks good.'

'We can't park there,' says Binky.

'Right, so you'll have to take us then,' says the camera assistant. 'Won't you, darling?'

'Yes, I was right,' says Joyce. 'No specs in the first scene.'

'Well done, Joyce,' says Simon. 'Right, Jules, one more take. You're doing brilliantly. But without the shades this time.'

'But they're my best pair,' says Jules. 'I bought them specially for the show.'

'Sorry,' says Simon. 'Back to the tree, if you don't mind. Right, everyone, let's go.'

'In our common room,' begins Jules again, slightly changing the words, though no one minds, 'we don't have smoking. It was a democratic rule – Oh shit, sorry about that.'

Raffy bursts out laughing. Simon stops the camera and goes across to talk to Jules.

'Just relax, take it easy. All we want you to do is tell us what you told us that first time, when you were taking us round.'

'I need my shades,' says Jules. 'I feel sort of stupid on my own. I need a sort of prop, something to do. Could I sort of look up at the helicopter?'

'No, that would be corny,' says Simon. 'And we'd really have to show it then.'

'It does make the school look very empty,' says Binky. 'Jules walking in the garden on his own, as if he was the only pupil. Couldn't someone walk behind him, perhaps saying "Hi" as he goes past? That would give him something to respond to.'

'I'll do it,' says Raffy, bounding forward. 'I could be walking here, like this, as if I've just come out of the common room, going the other way.'

'No thanks,' says Jules, quickly. 'I'll manage. That's the first time I've made a balls of it.'

'Hmm,' says Simon, thinking hard. 'It *would* look better. Yes, good idea, Binky. Okay then, Raffy. Ready, chaps? When I give you a sign, Raffy, just walk out of the door, and go past Jules on his left side. No need for you to say anything. Just keep walking, then disappear behind that tree.'

'When do I start walking?' asks Jules.

'At the same time as Raffy sets off,' says Simon. 'But we won't be seeing him then, only when he passes you. Right? On you go.'

Raffy starts off. As he passes Jules, with his back to the camera, he puts out his tongue and makes a stupid face, trying to put him off. Jules smiles, says hello, then goes into the beginning of his speech, heading for the door. He is totally relaxed and at ease, his best performance so far.

Before he reaches the tree, Raffy turns round to see what's happening, hoping Jules has made some mistake, and hoping to get his own face into the shot. He is walking while looking, which means he trips over the stick, the one stuck in the ground as Jules's marker. He stumbles, as if about to fall over, but just manages to regain his balance. Binky and Joyce start sniggering, expecting Simon to halt the camera, but he waves the crew on, not letting them stop. Jules comes into the common room, walks in the correct directions, completing his chat fluently and naturally, without making one mistake.

'Absolutely brilliant!' exclaims Simon. 'You're a natural, Jules. Right, that's a wrap. We'll have lunch now. Then we'll be back for just one more scene at two-thirty. Okay, chaps?'

The crew quickly pack up, while Simon and Binky confer. They are not going anywhere for lunch. Joyce is to get them a sandwich from Fred's Caff.

'Who's on your list of possibilities, Binky?' asks

100

Simon. 'We need something sort of chunky, a doing sort of scene. We've got enough talking, enough meetings and enough walkies. We could do with a bit of action.'

'Football,' says Raffy, coming across and butting in. 'I am the star of the football team. You must have heard that. I could get a team together this afternoon, pupils against staff, if you like. It'd be really good . . .'

'Thanks, Raffy,' says Simon. 'But not quite the sort of thing we can tie in with the National Curriculum.'

'I've got it,' says Binky. 'Hold on a moment.'

She dashes off across the common room, followed by Raffy.

Across the common room, around the couch

Colette and Kirsty see Binky coming their way and immediately start smiling, tossing their hair. Sam and Toby deliberately look the other way. Matt is deep into *Kerrang!*, going through the sections headed 'Kommunikation', 'Newz' and 'Komix'.

'Tell you what,' says Raffy, trying to hold Binky back. 'I could just do some training on my own. It is a bit late to set up a match. I can keep a football in the air a hundred times, you'll see. It would look great if you put some jokey music behind it. The *Grandstand* theme, or *Chariots of Fire* . . .'

'Hi,' says Binky, when she reaches the couch. 'Hope I'm not interrupting?'

'No, certainly not,' says Kirsty, all smiles. 'How's it going?'

'We've got on terrifically well all week, in fact. Done all the shots we planned. So well that Simon now thinks we might be able to fit in someone else this afternoon, perhaps one more sixth former, doing something interesting.'

'I did think of something,' says Colette. 'At least my mum did. Me and Kirsty go one afternoon a week to this old folks' home, to sort of help out. Well, we do it instead of Games. I forgot about that when you were asking us things.'

'Oh no, that would have been excellent,' says Binky. 'You should have said. But it's too late now. Such a shame.'

'In the gym then,' says Raffy. 'Me training on my own. Great sound effects.'

'It was actually Matthew I was interested in,' says Binky, standing before the couch. 'You are Matthew, aren't you?'

'Yeah,' says Matt. 'Thought you'd never ask. I got some notes in me pocket. Ten reasons why Maths is beautiful.'

'No, it was your motor car, actually, I wanted.'

'You what?' grunts Matt.

'It was you I saw yesterday, under the car?'

'What?' repeats Matt.

'It'll make a great shot,' says Binky. 'Just outside the school, you mending your car. One of the many activities of comprehensive students which might have to go, under the National Curriculum. I know from Mrs Potter that the school does offer Motor Mechanics.'

'That's just for fifth years,' says Colette. 'The

thickos who are leaving, to stop them wrecking the school.'

'Doesn't matter,' says Binky. 'Just what we need. It's such a beautiful-looking car as well.'

'It's at home,' says Matt.

'Is it working, though?'

'Yeah,' says Matt. 'But no petrol.'

'No problem,' says Binky. 'Joyce will give you some money. Just as long as you can get it here by two-thirty. Okay?'

'Yeah,' says Matt. 'But can I talk about Maths?'

'You can talk about anything you like, my sweet,' says Binky. 'But you will be under the car.'

Ella: very scornful

EPISODE 9

Later that day, the Cow and Bull

Everyone is celebrating in the pub. There's Simon and the crew, plus the nine sixth formers who have been so very helpful, even if they did not all appear in the film.

'When's it gonna be shown then, Si?' asks Raffy.

'In about four weeks, I think. I've got to do some final editing first on something else. Joyce will let you all know the TX date.'

'What?' asks Dim.

'Transmission date,' says Raffy. 'Don't you know anything?'

'Will you have to do much editing on this?' asks Toby.

'Not a lot,' says Simon. 'The advantage of video is that, in a way, you can edit as you go along.'

'I fancy going into telly,' says Raffy. 'Any jobs for me at your place, huh?'

'As an actor, of course,' says Jules. 'Your performance today was ace.'

'Yeah,' says Raffy. 'Glad you noticed that. I'd been working on it.'

'Like hell you had,' says Kirsty. 'We've all heard about it. You just fell over, trying to muscle in.'

'That was a pretend fall,' says Raffy. 'Fooled everybody. Er, will you leave it in, Si?'

'I hope so. It did look very, let's say, natural.'

'Actually, it's your job I'm after, not Jules's,' says Raffy. 'Couldn't be bothered with all that poncin' around. How did you start, Si?'

'I joined the BBC on one of their training schemes for graduates.'

'Where did you go?' says Raffy. 'Bleedin' Oxford?'

'Yes, actually,' says Simon. 'But there are lots of other ways of getting in. Binky was on a local paper before she joined the Beeb. You can start on the technical side, as a sound engineer. Or go in as a secretary, work your way up, move around, try different departments, different parts of the country. Once you're in, there are always lots of opportunities.'

'Yeah,' says Raffy. 'I'm probably gonna try the Oxbridge bit. The school is pushing me into it. Sounds boring and snobbish, but I suppose it would be a means to an end.'

'And what a boring, trivial end, ending up in the media,' says Ella.

'You think so?' says Simon, smiling indulgently.

'You just manipulate people, and the news,' says Ella. 'And in turn *you* get manipulated, by big business, or by the Government.'

'We try not to,' says Simon, still smiling, not wishing to get into any arguments.

'What's wrong with the media, Ella?' says Raffy. 'We can't all be brain surgeons. Or Florence Nightingale.'

'I think the media is important,' says Toby. 'You're wrong, Ella, to despise it. There's good and bad in every industry.'

'That's it,' says Raffy. 'It is an industry now. I was reading the other day, dunno where, the *Guardian* or *Kerrang!*, that the media will soon be a bigger industry than Industry.'

'How do you mean, Raf?' says Dim, getting interested.

'Well, I think that leisure and everything to do with it, tourism and stuff, is already the country's biggest employer, bigger than manufacturing. TV and the media, print and publishing and radio – that's coming up fast – they'll soon take over from heavy manufacturing.'

'There you are, then,' says Ella. 'The media is a symptom of modern society. Totally trivial. It's all materialism, or entertainment.'

'So what's wrong with that?' says Toby. 'We exported coal and ships and goods for centuries, now we're exporting culture.'

'That's true,' says Sam, pleased to hear Ella and Toby having different views for once.

'Yeah, but look at the culture,' says Ella. 'Pop music and stupid fashions.'

'Nothing wrong with fashion,' says Jules. 'I don't know why people knock it. Style is important.'

'Not that one again, Jules,' says Ella.

'So is pop music,' says Sam. 'I feel proud when you go abroad, round Europe, and it's all English pop music.'

'That's not the greatest thing,' says Raffy. 'We have got one big natural asset in this country, which happened by chance, really. Know what it is?'

'Amaze us, Raffy,' says Colette.

'English. You know, the English language.'

'When you gonna learn it, Raffy?' says Kirsty.

'Ha ha,' says Raffy. 'We're dead lucky, cos everyone else wants to learn English. It means we don't have to bother learning their languages.'

'But we should,' says Jules.

'That's another argument,' says Raffy. 'Let me finish. What's happened to those drinks, Joyce? Swallowed the purse, have you, darling?'

Simon tells her to order another round for everyone, then looks at his watch.

'Did you know,' continues Raffy, 'that America nearly spoke German?'

'What?' says Kirsty.

'When they were setting up the USA, they had this vote on which language to speak. English got it by only one vote. Otherwise it would have been German. That's true, isn't it, Simon?'

Simon nods his head, and checks his watch once again.

'Where was I?' says Raffy.

'Finished, I hope,' says Jules.

'You've had your turn, Jules,' says Raffy. 'All bloody week.'

'You're just jealous,' says Jules.

'Dead true,' says Raffy. 'Anyway, what I was gonna say was, cos of us having English, that's why our media does so well. It lets us flog all our books and our TV shows round the world. Just think, if you lived in a country with a boring little language, I dunno, Portugal or Armenia, you might be doing brilliant work, writing fantastic books or doing great programmes, but no one else will ever know. Unless it's really amazing. So we're lucky, see. We have an asset we have to capitalize on. No point manufacturing things any more. The Japanese do it better and cheaper.'

'But we've got to keep a balance,' says Ella. 'That's why we should subsidize coal and steel, if we have to. Why should people who have lived in a mining village for centuries be told they've had it and their life is being killed off?'

'That's the way it goes, ducky,' says Raffy. 'Life is cruel. Do you want yuppies in the City to be subsidized when the Stock Market next collapses? Course you don't. But it's just the same.'

'No, it isn't,' says Ella.

'I think you live in a fantasy world, Ella,' says Raffy. 'Not the real world. That's why I'm going into the media. It is the real world. The message is the medium. The medium is the message. So what about another drink? That's my main message.'

'Do you do any Media Studies in your school?' asks Binky brightly.

'Only the thickos,' says Raffy. 'You can do it as part of your CPVE course.'

'What's that?'

'Gawd, I thought you were the researcher,' says Raffy. 'Si, you wanna take me on now. I'll do your research for you. It stands for Certificate in Pre-Vocational Education. It's a one-year course for people not up to A levels, like what I am.'

'Yes, this is all most interesting,' says Simon.

Neville, the pub manager, appears with another very large round of drinks.

'I think there could be a programme in this one day,' says Simon. '*Sixth Formers Talking*. Don't you think so, Binky?'

'Super idea,' says Binky.

'Joyce, when you've settled up,' says Simon, 'we really have to be going. Love you and leave you. And thanks to all of you, you've been t'rific.' He goes round and shakes hands with everyone.

'Shame about Matt,' says Binky, as she too goes round shaking hands. 'But if you see him, tell him it didn't matter.'

Matt did not reappear in the afternoon, and has not been seen since. Instead, they managed to film a fifth-year Motor Mechanics group taking an old Cortina to pieces, which gave them the shots they wanted.

Joyce insists on shaking hands as well, followed

by the crew. Neville is most impressed by all this friendliness from a real TV crew, and has begun to think rather differently about Raffy and Co. Usually, he considers them a nuisance, buying so little but making so much noise.

After all the TV people have gone, leaving masses of empty glasses and bottles, Jules looks rather sad. 'Funny how in just a week,' he says, 'you become such friends. Even the crew. I got to know them all individually.'

'Yeah, you did,' says Raffy. 'And Ella and Taz and Dim. Okay for you four. Not for us. Not bloody fair.'

'I didn't want to get to know them,' says Ella. 'As for that Simon, condescending bastard. "*Sixth Formers Talking*".'

'Yes, that was a bit patronizing,' says Toby.

'I think it's a good idea,' says Raffy. 'And they're bound to pick me this time.'

'Yes, you were performing hard,' says Kirsty.

'Showing off, you mean,' says Colette.

'I was on form,' says Raffy. 'I should have charged them. Hey, did anyone of yous get paid?'

Jules looks a bit embarrassed. 'Well, actually, I was given £100, and signed some little form. It's some sort of facility fee, for using the common room. I'm going to give it to Mr Witting on Monday for the sixth-form fund.'

'You are bloody not,' says Raffy. 'That's our money. For the nine of us. Neville! Same again, squire. And make it snappy. You have got some real stars in tonight . . .'

Much later that night, closing time at the Cow and Bull

They all stagger out, laughing and shouting, pushing each other along the pavement. Even Ella has had a few drinks. She and Sam are walking home together. Dim is going back with Colette. Jules is seeing Taz home, as she lives not far from him. Raffy will see Kirsty home, so he says, as they live on the same estate. It looks as if Kirsty will have to see him home first, judging by Raffy's condition.

Outside the pub, they all kiss and cuddle and say their goodnights, then set off on their respective routes home. Raffy and Kirsty cross St Andrews Road. Halfway over, Raffy starts showing off, deciding to vault over a white Perspex bollard. A police car comes screaming past, heading north, just missing Raffy, but not stopping.

'Stupid driver!' shouts Raffy. 'I'm gonna report you to the police.'

He laughs loudly at this remark. Kirsty takes his hand, leading him safely across the pedestrian crossing to the other side. Jules is also being silly, doing a Fred Astaire dance round a lamppost on the other side of the road. Colette is pushing Dim and giggling at something she has said, making jokes about his tuckshop, suggesting a better name for it.

Raffy breaks away from Kirsty and goes back into the middle of the road, to have another go at the bollard. He manages to vault it properly this time, but his feet catch it slightly and it topples over. Another police car approaches, this time with its siren screeching. Raffy gives it a wave as it tears past.

'Not my fault,' he shouts, kicking the overturned bollard. 'It was dodgy. Blame Camden Council, not me.'

Kirsty comes for him again, drags him off the road, and keeps tight hold of his arm this time. Two more police cars can be heard in the distance, followed by an ambulance. Raffy puts his hands to his ears as they pass, going at a tremendous speed, in the same direction as the first police cars.

'There must be a police conference on somewhere,' says Raffy. 'Or a cop motor rally.'

'Don't be stupid,' says Kirsty. 'It's just another accident somewhere. They happen all the time.'

'Oh it's an exciting life in the modern police force,' says Raffy. 'I might have a go myself, if I don't get into the BBC.'

'Oh, hurry up,' says Kirsty, pulling him along the pavement. 'You won't be going anywhere, at this rate.'

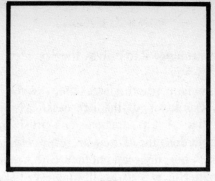

RIP

EPISODE 10

The common room, Monday morning

Kirsty and Colette are sitting on the couch. They have obviously been crying. All around the common room, there are little huddles of people, some standing and staring, others sitting and whispering.

'I've never known anyone dead before,' says Kirsty quietly. She rubs her eyes. 'He's the first dead person I know.'

They both stare into space, motionless, as if frozen, caught in mid-thought, mid-life.

'I can't believe it,' says Colette. 'I refuse to believe it. I think he's still alive. Somewhere.'

She looks at Kirsty, giving her a sad smile. They manage to exchange looks: weary, wintery, transparent looks. Then they burst into tears, holding on to each other. Nobody moves, nobody comes to comfort them or try and stop them crying. Everyone else wants to cry, or to display their own emotions some other way.

'I remember when I was about seven,' says Colette, eventually drying her eyes. 'My grandmother died. I was dragged to Carlisle by my mum, about this time of the year, really cold. I never really knew her, my grandmother. She was just an old woman. She was always ill whenever I saw her, always bad-tempered and moaning and telling people off. That's how she seemed to me. I was scared of her. Now, well, of course, I realize she was probably always in agony. Poor old sod.

'All I could really think about all day was this knickerbocker glory which my mum had promised me. After we'd been to the house, Mum said, we'll go to this Italian ice-cream parlour, which she always used to go to with her mum when she was my age. But first we were to go to my grandma's house, and pay our respects.'

Colette pauses, then smiles. 'I thought she did mean pay – you know, money – to have a look. As if it was somehow tied up with the knickerbocker glory.'

'And did you?'

'Did I what?' says Colette, abstracted, her mind still far away down childhood lanes, places she hasn't visited for a long time.

'Did you see her? Dead, I mean.'

'Oh yes,' says Colette. 'She was sort of laid out in her bed, in the front room, in her best nightdress. She looked lovely really. They'd put make-up on her face. She looked better than she did in real life.

'I wanted to touch her face. Awful, really, but I

was only seven. The skin looked real, but sort of realer, almost waxy.'

'Oooh, sounds horrible,' says Kirsty. 'Creepy. Imagine taking a little girl to look at a dead body. Cruel, I think.'

'My mum had read this article about facing death. How you must talk about it, not pretend it hasn't happened, make children face it, so they know it's real. Let them see that the person's body is gone, forever. You've got to let people grieve, that's the theory.'

'But didn't it give you nightmares?'

'Not really. But I suppose it was a pointless thing to do. My grandma didn't mean much to me, either way. All I thought about all day was the knicker-bocker glory I'd been promised.'

'And did you get it?'

'No, that was it,' says Colette, smiling. 'When we finally got there, the ice-cream parlour had closed over a year before. So naturally I stood outside and screamed and screamed, didn't I. Said I'd been cheated and it wasn't fair and all that . . .'

Kirsty smiles. Colette shakes her head.

'In all these years,' says Colette, 'I've never discussed that day with my mum. Funny, isn't it. Must have been something I blanked out.'

They both stare down at the carpet, lost in their own individual thoughts, of memories suppressed, things never spoken.

'Look,' says Kirsty. 'I think I can see the marks in the carpet. You know. Where Matt traced out that four-colour map thing.'

'Where?' says Colette. 'Oh God, I think I can as well.'

At the thought, they both burst into tears again.

Mrs Potter's office, later that day

Mrs Potter is sitting behind her desk, reading a letter. In front of her stand Colette, Kirsty, Sam, Ella, Jules, Dim and Raffy. They are grim and serious, looking down, not wanting to catch anyone's eye, patiently waiting for Mrs Potter to finish reading.

'I can understand your feelings,' says Mrs Potter, looking up, gazing at each of them, one by one. 'You're all in the same tutor group. And I know you've been in the same class as Matthew, all the way through school.'

They nod their heads. Ella rubs her eyes. Colette takes out a handkerchief. Jules coughs. Raffy swallows loudly.

'But it is clear from this letter that the family wants a very private funeral. He's going to be cremated on Wednesday. You can understand them wanting the minimum of fuss. So I think it would be best if none of you went along on Wednesday. I planned to go myself, with Mr Witting, but I think we should all respect the family's wishes.

'It's not quite clear, but his mother seems to be saying there might be a memorial service in a month or so. They are still thinking about it. That is very much the practice today. We shall see. He was so very young.

'A memorial service would give you an opportunity to pay your respects. In fact anyone from the sixth form would be welcome, I'm sure, should they want to go along. A memorial service tends to be a more joyous occasion, a public occasion, from my limited experience. It's a time when we remember the good things, the nice things, the happy things. Although, of course, a tragedy like this can never be forgotten.'

She looks up, gives each of them a little smile, then nods her head. The audience is over. She then picks up some other documents, consults another letter.

'Oh, Colette, as you're here. Perhaps you could inform your mother that the French department is going to arrange an exchange this year, possibly at Easter. I hope she'll think that's good news. And you as well, my dear.

'Oh, and Sam. That's lucky, you're here as well. This will save me writing to your father. We have now got the funds for the Geography field trip, so please tell him. Don't forget.'

'No, I won't,' says Sam.

'Thanks,' says Colette.

Then they all slowly file out of the Head's office.

Fred's Caff, not long afterwards

'What a woman,' says Ella. 'Going on about those stupid field-trip things. At such a time. She's no soul, that woman.'

'But what else can she do?' says Jules. 'Life has to go on.'

'And as for you saying "Thanks", Colette,' says Ella.

'I dunno why I said it,' says Colette. 'The word just came out.'

'What about Matt's mother?' says Sam. 'That's what I was thinking. Having to write that letter to Mrs Potter. When she must have so many things, and thoughts . . .'

They all sit silently. Ella takes Sam's hand and holds it.

'You're right,' says Ella. 'We're remote from it all really. And Mrs Potter is even more remote. She hardly knew him.'

'I thought about ringing his mother,' says Colette. 'Dunno why. I only met her once, after I'd spent that night in Matt's squat. What do you do in these cases?'

'Don't ring,' says Jules. 'They don't want that. Write if you must, that's the best thing. Just a note.'

'Have you written, Jules?' asks Ella.

'Yeah. Don't suppose she'll read it. They'll get so many. It was just for me I wrote it, I suppose, not to help her. How can you help?'

They all sit silently again. Raffy takes a mouthful of tea, slurping it, the noise of it going down his throat reverberating round the café. Normally, someone would shout at him. Instead, they look at each other, saying nothing. They know that their life is still going on, their normal, irritating, trivial old life. They all have it, all share it, unlike Matt.

'I've written as well,' says Raffy. They turn and look at him in obvious surprise.

'My gran said that was the thing to do. But not to expect a reply. So I said, don't reply.'

'What else did you say?' asks Kirsty.

'I just remembered a memory I had of Matt in the first year. We were in the school camp together. I was forced to share with him and I didn't really want to, cos you know what we thought of him at the time, a right drip, collecting stamps and all that, not here half the time, gone to lunch. But he was brilliant. We had a great time. Not one row in the whole week.'

'The thing about Matt,' says Jules, 'was that everyone liked him. He never said horrible things about other people. Never fell out with anyone. He was great, really. Wish I'd known him better. But you know how it is. You never think . . .'

They sit in silence once again.

'There's one thing that's amazed me,' begins Ella. 'Have you noticed? People going round saying they were his best friend, they sat with him, knew him all their life, went out with him. It's rather turned my stomach, some of these people grieving, all claiming part of him.'

'You shouldn't criticize people, Ella,' says Jules. 'Those are their feelings. They're entitled to them. We know who knew him, don't we? That's what matters.'

'But if you think about it,' says Colette, 'none of us really *did* know him. That's why he wasn't really in our gang, was he? Though I suppose we all gave Mrs Potter the opposite impression this afternoon, didn't we? . . . Just because he's in our class. Was in our class.'

'He still is,' says Raffy. 'That's how he'll always be. His life has stopped dead, wham, bam. We'll go on, and God knows what'll happen to us, but he'll be young for ever. We'll always remember him as he was. Everyone in the Sixth, whoever knew him, however slightly, will take his memory on with them till they die. I won't forget him. Cos he's the first person I've known, our age, sort of thing, who has died.'

'Yeah, me and Kirst were discussing that,' says Colette. They nod their heads.

'Makes life pretty meaningless,' says Ella. 'I mean, what's the point of it all? All our boring worries. Exams, parents, what we're doing Saturday night. All very petty, isn't it? When you think it might finish at any moment, for any of us.'

'Yeah, but that's how it's always been,' says Raffy, 'since it all began. Life is stupid, really. It's all a big con.'

'The thing about Matt's death,' says Sam, slowly, 'is that it should make you appreciate what you've got. Not depress you or make you more cynical, Raffy. We should be more aware that we are all alive. More thankful, thanks to Matt.'

'That is true,' says Ella.

'Makes me realize how silly we were over that stupid programme,' says Colette. 'Getting jealous and that, falling out, accusing each other. I was really depressed when I found out I wasn't in it. I gave my mother hell. Stupid, wasn't it? All out of proportion.'

Kirsty gives Colette a hug, and so does Ella.

'I wonder if it's a good thing that Matt wasn't in the programme in the end,' says Kirsty.

'How do you mean?' asks Colette.

'Well it would have been spooky to see him on the telly. Alive, when we know now he's dead.'

'Perhaps they would not have used the programme,' says Colette. 'Or cut him out.'

'I still think it was partly their fault,' says Ella.

'Not that again, Ella,' says Sam. 'He crashed his car cos he crashed his car. You can blame the icy road if you like, or him going too fast, his useless car or his rotten driving, but you can't blame them, just cos they paid for his petrol.'

'Are you going to tell Simon?' Ella asks Jules.

'Why should I?' says Jules. 'Doesn't really concern him. I don't think he ever met Matt.'

'The awful Binky did,' says Colette. 'But only once.'

'Anyway I don't care about the programme,' says Jules. 'Whether it goes out or not. I don't want to be famous any more. I just want to be alive . . .'

'Funny he was called Matthew,' says Kirsty. 'And loved Maths.'

'Beautiful,' says Colette.

And they all smile.

Will the television programme ever appear?
Find out in the next episodes of S.T.A.R.S.
And get ready to give a warm welcome to the
birth of *Sixth Sense*, an underground
sixth-form newspaper that tells it like it is.
But will the Head like it? And the parents?
Toby hopes so, but naturally Raffy has other
ideas, much to the embarrassment
of certain parties.

The books in the S.T.A.R.S. series

1. FIT FOR THE SIXTH

A new term, a new life in the sixth form at St Andrews
Road School. Enter Jules, the best dressed, Sam, looking
serious and trying to stand next to Ella, Colette, the mimic
and chocoholic, Dim, looking uncomfortable in his new
trainers, Raffy, loud-mouthed as ever and flirting with
Kirsty.

2. RAPPING WITH RAFFY

Being rich and famous is what it's all about – at least that's
what Raffy thinks. And the way he plans to make it is by
being a pop star. Pity he can't sing, dance or play any
instruments . . . Ella and her girlfriends decide to ignore his
giant ego – the combination of their plans and Raffy's
ambitions could be dramatic. Will there be tears and
tantrums, or will someone find fame and fortune?

3. SHE'S LEAVING HOME

Colette and her mother are forever arguing. If it's not about
Colette's future, it's about her mother's boyfriend. Or her
mother's high-heeled shoes. Or her mother's tight jeans.
Parents' night at St Andrews Road School makes Colette
cringe, but being accused by her mum of pinching money is
the last straw.

4.   PARTY, PARTY

The sixth-form Christmas party has all been planned – the disco, the food, the booze – when it turns out banned. Raffy's fault, of course. He and the football team wrecked the common room, after post-match drinkies with the opposition. But suddenly it's chunky, hunky, clever old Dim who steps up, to make the day, and a bit of money . . .

5.   ICE QUEEN

Taz is elegant, exotic and elusive. She's been at S.T.A.R.S. for almost a term now, but still no one knows her, or her secrets. So what a challenge, especially for our Raffy. He knows he's witty and sexy and charming, as he's told everyone. But he can't get this message across to Taz when she won't even talk to him. But he is able to help out with her family troubles and at last he has a chance to start melting the Ice Queen . . .

7.   WHO DUNNIT?

It's never dull at S.T.A.R.S. but recently things have been heating up. That's why Toby has come up with his great idea – what S.T.A.R.S. needs is a magazine. But no one else shares his enthusiasm. Raffy thinks it'll be dead boring, Kirsty's too busy to help and Sam's being a wimp. Then an anonymous article is posted through Toby's door and everything is suddenly different.

8. A CASE OF SAM AND ELLA

Ella is worried. She thinks she might be pregnant. What will she tell Sam, what about her parents and her future? Sam is useless, as usual. He is distracted, scared stiff that Vinny, the school yob, is out to get him. Sam doesn't know why. He's never done anything to harm Vinny – or has he? And as for his stomach pains, well, what did he ever do to deserve such agony – and why doesn't anybody believe him? Is he really faking it?

9. THE FRENCH CONNECTION

S.T.A.R.S. sixth formers are taking part in a French exchange. When the French arrive they want to see the bright lights and Dim is the only one who can give them a good time. In Paris, Colette thinks her French family have a madman in the attic, but it looks like Raffy is finally in with a chance.

10. PLAYING AWAY

What's got into Taz and Toby? They're holding hands and gazing into each other's eyes . . . in a muddy field in Dorset, of all places. What sparked it off? And what is the connection between Taz and little Fen, the first former who hooks on to Toby and then mysteriously disappears? And as for disappearing, will Sam have to leave London?

11. LET'S STICK TOGETHER

When certain items go missing at St Andrews, the search is on for the culprit. Raffy's been acting suspiciously for some time now and seems a natural choice for questioning. Has he really gone too far this time? What will happen to him? And what will happen to S.T.A.R.S. anyway, if the governors opt out of local education? Will it be the end of St Andrews as we know it?

12. SUMMER DAZE

What's everyone doing for the summer holidays? Lucky Toby and Taz are heading for the sun, but what about the rest of the group? How will they survive without each other? Or will they have to?

EVERY COPY SOLD FIGHTS DRUG ABUSE

Every time you buy a copy of S.T.A.R.S. a donation goes to TACADE, a charity nationally recognized as the leading organization working in the field of alcohol and drug education.

TACADE, the Advisory Council of Alcohol and Drug Education, believes that education is vital to fight against drug abuse and that prevention in this way is the only long-term hope.

TACADE educates by offering you and your teachers resource materials, advice and support from professionals and, wherever possible, in-service training.

To do all this, TACADE needs money, as they can only prevent more alcohol and drug abuse as far and as fast as money is provided.

HOW WILL YOUR MONEY BE SPENT?

The money raised for TACADE will be spent on a health education programme for children in primary schools, so that when they are older, they will KNOW to say NO.

AND HOW YOU CAN HELP WITH THE FUNDRAISING

Apart from reading the S.T.A.R.S. series, and so donating to this charity, you can do more to help TACADE *and* have a great time doing it.

Why not organize a fund-raising disco in your school, with your teacher's permission? A special party pack is available to make the event both fun and worthwhile. For this and any other information or help, please contact TACADE, (Party Kit Offer), 3rd Floor, Furness House, Trafford, Salford, Manchester M5 2XJ. Telephone: (061) 848 0351.